The Girls of S

Book 2

Catherine Jones

Contents

CHAPTER ONE

The early morning sunlight glistened across the water, creating golden streams of light that stretched out as far as the eye could see. Mac yawned as she walked around the corner of the deck, sitting down on one of the teal plastic chairs to eat her cereal. Eating breakfast on the deck had become her morning routine since moving into the apartment above Russo's with Emma and Mads, she loved the smell of the fresh salt air and the sound of the seagulls searching for their morning meals in the cove.

"Here you go, Sammy," she said as she threw Cheerios to the one-legged seagull that was perched in his usual spot on the deck.

"Good morning, Mac!"

Mac waved to Jim Sousa, who walked his two dogs, Mike, and Mark, around the cove every morning. Both dogs looked up at Mac and barked, as if to say hello, before focusing on a Dalmatian and its owner that was heading their way.

"Did Mads come home last night?" Emma asked, offering Mac a piece of avocado toast as she sat down next to her.

"No, she worked late," Mac replied, looking at Emma and then bursting into laughter.

"Oh right, right. *Working*," Emma air quoted, laughing. "I'd be working late all the time, too, if I had a handyman that looked like Rylan."

As if on cue Mads pulled up into the cove in Rylan's Jeep, parking below the deck in front of Russo's. The top and doors of the Jeep were off of it, a signal to Mac to drop a few pieces of her cereal onto Mads head from above.

"What the…?" Mads said as she picked the pieces out of her messy bun, looking up. "I guess that's what I get for parking here!"

She hopped out of the vehicle, her tanned, honey brown skin emphasized by the cropped white tank top and cut off distressed white jean shorts that she was wearing. A few minutes later she appeared on the deck, her sunglasses perched on top of her head.

"Well, well, well, look what the cat dragged in," Mac joked. "Want some?"

"No thanks," Mads said, shaking her head no at the bowl of cereal that Mac was holding out towards her. "I ate the ones you threw at me."

"Hard night at work?" Emma asked Mads, winking at Mac.

"Yes, actually. The final upgrades on the second floor are done and we just needed to go through and make a punch list of anything that might have been missed."

"Who is we? You said *we* needed to go through, did you have a mouse in your pocket or something?" Mac teased as Emma laughed.

"The mouse's name is Rylan," Emma joked, hi-fiving Mac.

"Oh my God, stop. Just because Rylan's a nice-looking guy it doesn't mean that we are hooking up," Mads eyerolled.

"Well, it doesn't mean that you aren't either," Emma joked.

"Gonna be a hot one today, girls! Make sure you drink plenty of water. Mac, do you know if the store has more of those strawberry smoothie drinks that your mom was making yesterday? They are so refreshing!"

"Yes, they're available every day, Mrs. Swayne," Mac yelled down to the woman, standing up so she could see her better. "Tell her to add some banana to it, you'll love it."

"I'll be there in about fifteen minutes for my shift, just come see me and I'll whip one up for you," Emma added.

"Oh! Banana! That sounds delicious. Thank you! Emma, I will see you soon. Take care, girls."

"Bye Mrs. Swayne!" all three girls said at the same time, waving to the elderly woman. She was a well-known local who practiced meditation every morning in the cove on the large rocks that overlooked the water, where she would sit for an hour humming and chanting.

The girls all walked into their apartment, Mac leaving the slider door open so the breeze from the ocean could enter the space.

"We really need a screen door for this," she said, knocking on the glass slider. "Yesterday a beetle the size of my hand flew in here."

"I can have Rylan put one in," Mads said as she flopped down on the chaise part of the large sofa sectional the trio had bought for the apartment.

"Mads, do you want the rest of this avocado toast?" Emma asked." I have to get going to work."

"Absolutely not. Avocado is so gross Emma, I have no idea how you eat it. Blech."

"It's good for you," Emma said as she wrapped her long, cherry red hair up into a top knot.

Mac didn't know if it was all of the avocado toast that Emma was eating but over the last few weeks she had looked radiant. Her skin had a golden glow with a smattering of freckles thanks to the summer sun, and her hair was thick and shined like glass. She had gained weight, which had been needed because she'd been far too thin when Mac had first come back from California four months ago. Whatever Emma was doing was working, Mac liked seeing her so happy and healthy.

"I'll stick to my same breakfast routine, thanks. Pretzels washed down with a Diet Coke followed by iced coffee all day has worked wonders for my figure," Mads joked.

"I'm surprised you came here instead of staying at the resort, aren't you sitting in on the meeting that I have with your parents today in half an hour?" Mac asked Mads.

Even though Mads lived with Mac and Emma, she'd been spending half of the week, if not more, overnight at her parent's resort. At first Mac had assumed it was because Emma and Mads shared a bedroom, and maybe Mads wanted time alone some nights, but she had soon realized that Rylan, the handyman for the resort who had arrived in the spring, played a role in Mads wanting to spend the night at the resort. Rylan had a room there all summer, and he'd become one of Mads' summer flings, although Mac could see this being a long-term relationship. Emma could, too, but any time they brought it up to Mads she would roll her eyes and change the subject.

"No. Babs and Dick said they wanted to meet with you alone. They probably want to tell you how bad of a job I'm doing with the reno's, how over budget I am. Put in a good word for me, would ya?" Mads asked, sliding down on the chaise and pulling the mirrored sunglasses off of her head and down over her eyes.

"Do you want a ride, I'm leaving now," Emma asked Mac.

"No thanks, I've got a meeting after I meet with Mads parents."

"Okay. Could you drop these bags off at the resort store for me? It'd save me the trip later on," Emma asked, nodding at two bags sitting on the floor next to the front door.

"Sure, no problem," Mac said. She went to her room and changed into the clothes that she had laid out on her bed after she'd showered earlier, a pair of navy blue cropped linen wide leg pants and a white sleeveless v neck button-down silk shirt. She took her bag, grinning as she heard Mads snoring in the living room and hurried out the door.

****

The Sandy Shore Resort was buzzing, which was the standard for a hot August morning at the beach. There were dozens of people on the beach already, some getting a morning walk in and others claiming their spot on the beach for the day. Mac held the glass door open for a large family of six that was on their way to do the latter, the father pulling a massive cooler and the kids all carrying floats and snorkels while the mom made a feeble attempt to spray them each with sunblock.

Once she was inside the resorts large lobby she dropped off the beach bags that Emma had asked her to, waving to Brian and Jenn, who worked at the front desk. She had gotten close with the entire front desk staff during her time working there, they'd been hesitant when she had told them they were moving to all online reservations but now that they had gotten used to using the new system they loved it.

"Looking good, Tommy," she joked as she walked past the janitor, who was mopping the lobby floor. Because of the resorts beach front location, it was impossible to keep the lobby floor sand free, but Tommy tried the best that he could.

"Right back at ya, Mac!" Tommy said cheerfully as Mac opened the door to the office.

"Mac! As always, you are right on time," Mad's father, Dick, said. "Take a seat."

Mac sat down at the small round table that was in the office as Mad's mother, Barb, walked in.

"Hi Mac, I brought you one of those whipped coffee creations from your parent's store. I'm a bit addicted, I have to admit."

Mac laughed as Barb placed the large plastic cup down on the table.

"I think the whole town is addicted," Mac laughed as she took the large plastic cup from Barb. "Thank you."

"Well, let's start, shall we?" Dick asked, looking at his watch.

Mac pulled out the eight-page report that she had written up the day before, handing a copy to each of them. She watched as Barb and Dick looked over the report, their facial expressions ranging from surprise to shock to, well, she wasn't sure, but thought it could be disappointment.

"This is very thorough," Dick said.

"I tried to cover everything possible. The renovations delayed it, as we discussed."

"Oh, we understand. That was actually a good thing, that you were here when we started, I mean. Just the suggestion to add a fully stocked minibar geared towards families in each room was something we never would have done," Barb said." At least not with your ideas, the snack variety."

"Those little fridges provide a nice profit every week. I said no to having them in the rooms when we first opened up, now I'm kicking myself for not doing it," Dick said.

"The families love them. They wipe them out each stay, actually some are almost daily. It's easier for them to grab a snack in the room then take the kids out. Oh, and the toys? That's been a big seller also. Personally, I am almost embarrassed to charge what we do for them, but again, looking at the numbers almost every family buys them," Barb said.

Mac had suggested leaving beach themed items in the rooms, things like extra-large beach blankets and large plastic buckets filled with sand molds, balls, and toys. If guests chose to use them they were charged extra each day, or they could buy them. The price they charged just for one day's use covered their purchase cost, so it was all profit after that.

"I'm glad it's worked out. If you look at the last page of the report, I've only got one more area that I think can be improved. As mentioned last month, the space in the lobby next to the store could be used for revenue. I'm not sure exactly what could be placed there, though, because of how narrow it is. The store does a good business, but I don't think enlarging it by knocking the wall down would necessarily bring more money in because there's really no more items that you need to carry there, and it'd be a waste to use just for storage."

Barb and Dick looked at each other, Barb shifting in her seat uneasily and tapping her pen on the table.

"Of course, it's up to you to make that decision, and it isn't urgent or anything. It could wait until next year, or just leave it as is," Mac said, realizing that they'd made a lot of changes over the past few months, all based on her recommendations, and it had been far from cheap.

"Oh no, we agree with you. We've talked about it since you first mentioned it a month ago, and in talking to Rylan it seems that he can make it into a usable space fairly fast," Dick explained. "He's actually already started."

"We already have an idea for the space, and a person to rent it," Barb said, looking from Dick to Mac.

"Oh. Well, that's great!" Mac replied enthusiastically, unsure why they seemed to be nervous. "What will the space be used for?"

"I had the idea when I was down in Portsmouth getting my nails done. It's such a hassle, the drive and all. When I looked at the space I realized that it's just a bunch of stations in a row, which can easily fit in the space we have here."

"So, the space is going to be a nail salon?" Mac asked.

"Yes. Tracy Simkin has agreed to rent it out to start hers. I know there was an issue between her and Emma in the past, and as far as I know that's all over with, so I assume there's not going to be any issues, right?" Barb asked.

"I told her to talk to you and Madison before she went out and promised anything, but she didn't listen to me," Dick said, shaking his head.

"Oh, stop. It will be fine. These aren't little kids anymore, they're adult women. This is business! It will be fine!" Barb said excitedly.

Mac forced a smile as she nodded her head in agreement, but inside she was cringing, and she wasn't nearly as positive as Barb that everything would be fine.

CHAPTER TWO

Walsh's Market on Main was buzzing, which
had become the norm for the popular store, thanks to
Mac's changes. As expected, the addition of coffee and
fresh baked goods, along with more popular seasonal
items, had been a hit with the locals and vacationers, as
had the outdoor seating. The store was always full,
which was no surprise to anyone. Thanks to having one
of the best locations in town it provided the perfect spot
to people watch, one could grab a coffee and muffin
and watch the parade of beachgoers walk by. In the
evenings it was just as popular thanks to the selection
of desserts they had started to carry, people would go
out to eat dinner and then walk to the store for a bit of
exercise and reward themselves with a frosted brownie
or freshly made cannoli.

"Good morning ladies, hello Lyle," Mac said to Verna Nixon and Deb Hilare, locals, and Verna's dog Lyle, who was sitting at Verna's feet at one of the tables outside. The two women met there every morning at nine, each of them eating a muffin while people watching and gossiping about the latest happenings in Summer Cove.

"Mac, your hair color is just so refreshing! The blonde highlights are so pretty. Every time I see you I am reminded of my younger years," Deb sighed, as Verna let out a laugh.

"Well Verna, the difference is Mac's hair color is natural and yours came from Betty at Salon Cutters in Portsmouth!"

The two women laughed, and Mac grinned as she entered the store.

"Emma, I'll take that smoothie now, dear."

"Coming right up, Mrs. Swayne," Emma said, nodding her head hello to Mac as she approached her.

"I'll take one too, please. I have a long drive ahead of me," Mac said to Emma, smiling at Mrs. Swayne. "After you make Mrs. Swayne's, of course."

Mrs. Swayne nodded her head in acknowledgement, and Mac grinned as she looked around the busy store. People were buying a variety of items, some were picking up fresh fruits and vegetables, and most also took home some of the fresh eggs that were a big hit. Then there were vacationers who needed more sunblock or a boogie board, and the ones who had just arrived for the week were stocking up for their house rental with paper plates, water and soda, and assorted cereals and snacks.

Her parents had hired on Emma as well as a few other locals, and Emma had stepped up and basically ran the store for the most part, at least Mac thought that she did. She knew that her parents had a tough time giving up control, but they also had slowed down since her dad's accident. Mac was grateful that Emma liked working there, if she didn't it would have meant that Mac would need to be there a lot more and that wasn't anything Mac was interested in. The customers loved Emma, she was a people person and did a fantastic job.

"Almost done."

Mac turned to Emma, considering telling her what she'd just learned about Tracy's nail salon. She had to tell her, she didn't want Emma to hear it from anyone else. But this wasn't really the time or place, the store was full, and once she told Emma, Emma might want to leave work, and Mac didn't want to cause any drama.

"Don't you have an important meeting?"

Mac turned to her mother, who was looking at the clock on the wall.

"Hi mom, good to see you too," Mac joked as she gave her mom a peck on the cheek. "I'm leaving now. I just needed a smoothie for the ride. Thanks Emma," she said. "I'll talk to you later, mom."

She left the store, putting her sunglasses on as she made her way to the car. The heat was really rolling in, she hoped the traffic wasn't too bad.

****

Mac fanned her face with her hand as she pulled up the long driveway, cursing the broken air conditioning in the old Toyota. The Van Rohrer's, her potential new client, had asked that they meet at their house, which was an hour's drive from Summer Cove. It was ninety-two degrees outside and opening the windows hadn't helped cool her down at all on the drive there.

"Good Lord," she said aloud as she saw the house, a massive Mediterranean style home set behind a circular driveway that had a large water fountain in the middle of it. There were arches and balconies galore. She had assumed that the Van Rohrer's would have a big house, they were multi-millionaires after all, but this was much larger than what she had envisioned. It reminded her of some of the houses that she'd seen on one of The Real Housewives shows that she and Emma and Mads liked to watch.

After parking her car across from the front door, she turned the rearview mirror towards her so she could freshen up her makeup. She was pleasantly surprised that her makeup hadn't melted down her face, the tinted moisturizer that Mads had given her held up well in the heat and her liquid eyeliner and mascara were waterproof, which she assumed meant sweatproof as well but wasn't positive. Her hair was a thick bundle of curls, thanks to the sea salt spray that she had started to use. It eliminated frizz and brought out her natural curls, all she needed to do was run some serum through her dried hair once or twice a day to keep it looking good.

Picking up her padfolio from the passenger seat she opened the car door, groaning as a wave of humidity hit her, and stood up, fluffing her blouse out a bit as it was clinging to her lower back. Taking a deep breath, she walked towards the front door.

As she stood at the door she hesitated, looking from the large gold door knocker that was on it over to the doorbell that was on the side. She opted for the doorbell, pressing the button, and could hear it echo inside the house for a few seconds before the door opened up.

"Mackenzie?" an older woman who was dressed in all black asked. Her grey hair was pulled into a tight bun, and her tanned skin was heavily wrinkled which led Mac to think that this wasn't Mrs. Van Rohrer. She imagined that someone with as much money as the Van Rohrer's had would lean towards Botox and anything else that would slow the aging process, or make it appear so anyway.

"Yes, I'm Mackenzie Walsh, I'm here to see the Van Rohrer's."

"Miss Walsh, nice to meet you. I'm Jemma, the Van Rohrer's house manager. Please, come in."

Mac stepped inside the house, squinting as the natural light poured through the windows into the large two-story foyer. A double sided, curved staircase led to the second floor. The staircase was enormous and had intricate carvings along it, complete with the letters V and R etched in the center.

"This is beautiful," Mac said as she walked behind Jemma.

"The Van Rohrer's have very good taste," Jemma said in agreement as she led Mac to a door directly off of the foyer, then down a flight of stairs and through a narrow hallway. She knocked on the last doorway in the hall before opening it up, revealing a large room that served as the Van Rohrer's office.

The space had two large cherrywood desks across from each other, along with a large eight-person conference table and a smaller round table that could seat four, both also in cherrywood. There was a glass wall that looked out onto the back yard, displaying a massive in ground pool surrounded by Arborvitae trees that had to be close to twenty feet high.

"This is Miss Mackenzie Walsh," Jemma announced to the Van Rohrer's, who were both sitting at their desks, before turning and shutting the door behind her.

"Nice to meet you Mr. and Mrs. Van Rohrer," Mac said with a smile as she approached them, her arm extended for a handshake.

"Please, call us Mandy and Bob if you'd like. Thank you for coming, Mackenzie. I hope the drive wasn't too bad, the summer vacationers flood the streets, it seems to get worse every year," Mrs. Van Rohrer said. From the research that she had done, Mac knew Mandy Van Rohrer was fifty-nine, but she didn't look a day over forty. Her skin was dewy and smooth, and her sleeveless shirt revealed toned arms that reminded Mac that she really needed to hit the gym.

"It wasn't too bad. I grew up in Summer Cove so I'm accustomed to the summer traffic. You grew up here in Bristol as well, I believe?"

"Yes, both Bob and I did. That's how our flagship store came to be here in this town," Mandy said, gesturing for Mac to sit down across from them at the large round table.

"Mackenzie, we visit your parents store a few times a year, we like to drive along the coast and Summer Cove is always one of our stops. When we stopped by in June we couldn't believe the transformation that had taken place, it's like a new store yet it still has the charm of the old one. I asked who did the changes, and that's how I got your information. Our business needs help. A facelift of sorts," Bob explained to Mac.

"Well, I can certainly help you with that, and thank you for the feedback about my parent's store. It was important for us to keep the charm from past years while stepping into the current one. What do you have in mind for changes, what's your goal?" Mac asked, taking her pen out as she flipped the padfolio open.

"We're hoping that maybe you can tell us," Mandy sighed. "We've tried to get the General Manager to step up, but so far they haven't. Meanwhile our revenue keeps going down every year. Our competitors are all doing well, Home Goods and TJ Maxx for example. I think the difference with them is they've adapted to current times, and we haven't, we are still the same Van Rohrer's from years ago."

Mac nodded her head that she understood as she wrote down her notes. Van Rohrer's was well known along the east coast, they had fifteen stores between Florida and Maine. Her mother loved shopping there for the same reason a lot of people did, they had name brands for less. The issue was that the name brands they sold were popular decades ago, not necessarily now.

"I'd need to see the store to be able to write up my proposal," Mac said.

"Well, that sounds fantastic. How fast can you do this, get us a proposal?" Bob asked.

"As you can tell, my husband is very eager to start," Mandy joked. "I can take you to the store here in town whenever it works for you."

"Actually, I'd prefer to go alone, that way the staff doesn't know who I am. Part of the experience is based on how your employees work, so I wouldn't want them to know that I'm there to assess them. I'd just be an ordinary customer. I'll take notes on my phone, so they'll just assume I am texting someone."

"Oh, I see. That makes sense. Well then, you can go whenever you want," Mandy said.

"Can you go today?" Bob asked.

"Bob! I am sure we aren't her only customer!" Mandy said, rolling her eyes at him.

"Actually, I can go today. Right now, in fact," Mac said, hoping she wasn't coming across as desperate. She didn't have any other customers aside from Mads parents and she didn't want to appear desperate to the Van Rohrer's, but her work at the Sandy Shore was almost done. "Since I am up here in town it works out well."

"Well, then this is perfect. When can we expect your proposal?" Bob asked.

"Well, that depends on what I see. It could be a day, or a week, depending on the research I may have to do."

"Research?" Mandy asked.

"Yes. As an example, the Sandy Shore Resort is my client. I've worked with them over the summer on several things, one of which was rooms. The décor, amenities, all of that. I researched what the top resorts in the United States offer in their rooms, as well as the top resorts along the east coast, and then obtained pricing on certain items that I recommended. That way they know how much this will cost, and I also project the increase in revenue and profit from it."

"Well, that's very thorough. We look forward to getting your proposal, Mac," Bob said, standing up and extending his hand. "The sooner the better."

"Mac, let me walk you out," Mandy said as Mac shook Bob's hand before the two women left the room.

"I apologize if my husband seems too pushy. He is just eager to get this started, it's something we should have done ages ago."

"No worries, I understand," Mac said. "I'll try and turn around my proposal as fast as I can. The store is along the main road here in town, correct?"

"Yes, it's only ten minutes down the road. It was nice to meet you Mac, I hope we'll be working together on this soon."

Mac shook Mandy's hand and then walked to her car, feeling a bit embarrassed as Mandy watched her get into the old beat-up vehicle and drive away. The Van Rohrer's cars weren't in the driveway, but Mac was positive that whatever cars they owned, they had air conditioning.

She drove to the location and pulled into the parking lot slowly, taking note of the outside of the store. It was pretty bland, a standard tan colored building with the Van Rohrer's signature logo, the letters VR, at the top of it. The large windows were bare, as was the sidewalk in front of the building.

The blast of cold air from the air conditioning was a welcome relief once she was inside the store, and she walked to where the carriages were lined up and pulled one out. As she started to push it one of the wheels locked up, making a screeching noise. She kicked it with her toe, but it was jammed, and she dragged it back to pick another one, only to find that one had some kind of sticky liquid on the handle part. The third time was the charm, and she pushed the metal carriage into the store, pausing as she looked around.

Mac remembered going school shopping there with her mother when she was younger, although it had seemed different back then. She remembered everything being organized, the clothes neatly hung on the racks and the shoes displayed with a pair on top of boxes that held varied sizes.

This store wasn't like that. The racks of clothes were jammed in next to each other too tightly, with too many clothes on each one so that if you wanted to look at something you had to remove it from the rack. This had resulted in clothes that people didn't want lying on top of the rack, empty hangers on the floor, clothes falling off of hangers. The shoe section had mismatched shoes together, shoes that had been tried on lying on the floor in the aisles, and empty boxes lying out on the aisle floor. It looked sloppy.

Mac wrote down notes in her phone as she slowly walked up and down the aisles, taking pictures as well.

The home goods section was as unorganized as the other sections, with bed sheets stuffed in between glassware and fake plants. Her carriage got stuck on a piece of the broken linoleum floor, something that clearly needed to be replaced.

As she walked up and down the aisles she typed into her phone, noting the not so current designers that were being sold and the changes that she wanted to recommend. Taking pictures helped as well, she could compare what the space looked like better from the pictures than her memory when she was recommending the new layouts in her proposal.

Before finishing she paused to look around again, taking a few more pictures of the store from the entrance.

"Can I help you?"

She jumped, startled.

"No, thanks," she replied, turning to look at the man that had asked. He was about her age, tall, with short sandy blonde hair and cheekbones that looked like they could cut glass. His dark blue eyes matched the color of his shirt, which didn't have a nametag on it like all of the other employees did.

"Uh, okay then," he said in an annoyed tone, walking away towards the returns desk, where a pretty blonde stood giggling and batting her extra-long eyelashes at him.

Mac left the store, adding onto her notes that employees having their significant others hang out at work shouldn't be allowed, it was unprofessional. She didn't want to get anyone in trouble, that wasn't what she was there to do, but she knew the Van Rohrer's wouldn't like seeing it either.

CHAPTER THREE

"Can I borrow these?"

Mac looked at the gold necklaces in varying lengths that Mads was already wearing. They had been gifts from Austin, and in some way she felt that if she wore them it was disrespectful to Rigsy, so they had just sat in her jewelry box for the past few months.

"Sure. They look good on you."

"Thanks. I love layered necklaces. How'd your meeting with my parents go?"

"Uh, well, it was interesting," Mac said as she sat down on the couch, refreshed after taking a shower and changing into a pair of shorts and a T-shirt. The ride home from the Van Rohrer's store had been almost two hours thanks to traffic, and she'd been a sweaty mess by the time she'd arrived at home.

"Uh oh," Mads said. "Interesting doesn't sound good. Or is it?"

"We talked about the new space they have, the small narrow one next to the store in the end of the lobby."

"Okay. Why is this some kind of big secret, the space? It isn't like I don't know about it I walk by it two hundred times a day. It was dumb of them not to have it used for the store when they built it to begin with. Now they've been acting weird about it, I saw them outside of it yesterday and they practically ran when they saw me walking towards them."

"It's going to be a nail salon," Mac said.

"It is? Well, that's not the worst idea, really. The way they were acting all secretive about it I figured it was going to be something like a timeshare office. You know, one guy sitting at a desk trying to sucker people into buying a week at the resort for the rest of their life. Then again, I don't think that's really suckering people in, it'd probably be good if they come every year anyway, right?"

"Uh, Mads, hello? Think about what I just said," Mac said to her friend, trying to steer her back to the original subject.

"You said a nail salon. What's the big deal?" Mads asked, spooning some ice cream into a bowl before stopping and looking at Mac. "OH WAIT. OH, HECK NO!"

"Oh, heck yes," Mac said, her eyes opened wide as she looked at Mads. "Apparently, Tracy already has an agreement with your parents."

"Why would they do this without even talking to me? Or you? I mean, you're the one who's in charge of all of this stuff. Shouldn't they have had you run numbers or whatever it is you do?"

"Well, I kind of already did," Mac said, sighing. "I told them what they could rent the space out for during the season. So, I guess maybe they just went with that number."

"That doesn't explain how they wound up renting it to Tracy. Wouldn't they need to run an ad or something, that the space is available to rent? This town is so small, how would we not hear about this?"

Mac agreed that it was odd that neither she nor Mads had heard about this from the rumor mill. Unless, of course, the rumor mill didn't know, which would be next to impossible in this town.

"Oh wait. I know. Her parents," Mads said matter of factly.

"Huh?" Mac asked.

"I bet this happened because my parents are friendly with Tracy's. They must have been out at dinner or playing golf or whatever, and this space came up, and it just went from there."

Mac nodded her head slowly in agreement, knowing that Mad's parents were good friends with Tracy's. They were friendly with almost all of the locals, including Mac's parents.

"That makes sense. I guess overall it doesn't matter how it happened, I'm more worried about how we tell Emma," Mac said.

"How you'll tell me what?" Emma asked as she walked through the front door. Mac cringed, realizing that with the slider and windows open you could hear the conversations inside of their apartment from outside in the stairway and landing that led to their front door.

"Uh, Mac has something to tell you," Mads chickened out, looking from Emma to Mac as she carried her bowl of ice cream over to the couch.

Mac shot Mads a dirty look as Emma walked over to the couch and sat on the wide arm that was at the end of it.

"Is this about the store?" Emma asked. "Because your parents have been acting kind of weird lately."

"No, it's nothing about the store. It's about the Sandy Shore," Mac said, trying to think of how she was going to tell her friend about the nail salon.

"The Sandy Shore? What does that have to do with me?" Emma asked, looking from Mads to Mac. "Can you just tell me what is going on?"

"Tracy is opening her nail salon inside the Sandy Shore," Mac blurted out, as Mads cringed.

"Oh," Emma said, tilting her head sideways. "Hmph. A nail salon at the resort. Hmm. Well, I guess that's good for the guests, but kind of stupid since it isn't open year-round."

Mac watched as Emma stood up and walked into the kitchen, looking inside the refrigerator.

"Well, that definitely wasn't the reaction I expected," Mac whispered to Mads, who slowly nodded her head in agreement as the two looked at Emma, who was pulling assorted items out of the fridge.

"Guys, it's fine," Emma said as she made herself a sandwich. "Tracy and Mark broke up, remember? And even if they were still together I wouldn't care. She was bound to open that stupid nail salon somewhere, it was just a matter of time for her to find a space in town."

"I just thought you might be mad that someone we knew was the one renting the space to her," Mac said.

"Uh, yeah and that's because you told my parents to rent that space out!" Mads said defensively. "It's been there forever, I'm pretty sure my parents could have lived without throwing carpet down and Rylan building it out, all so my parents could make a whopping few extra thousand dollars a year."

"I didn't tell them to rent it to Tracy, Mads. And your parents paid me to find ways to make their resort more money. I was just doing my job."

"Guys, stop. Your parents run a business, Mads. This isn't personal. Your mom buys a lot of my beach bags, she's been super supportive of me. Like Mac said, she was just doing her job. She didn't specifically say it was the perfect space for a nail salon. It's a long, narrow space with a door that's sat empty forever. I mean, I remember hiding in it when we were just kids playing hide and go seek. Seriously guys, I appreciate that you are looking out for me, but this isn't a big deal to me."

Mac watched as Emma finished making the sandwich, trying to see if she was just saying that she was okay when in fact she was upset. Whenever Emma was upset she would bite the inside of her cheek, which was easy to see because her face would shift, her lips moving to one side. That wasn't happening, nor was she stopping to bite her nails, something else she did when she was upset. Satisfied that Emma really wasn't upset Mac sighed with relief and opened her laptop up.

She'd worried all day over nothing. Emma was fine.

****

Mac made her way through the crowd that was standing outside of Russo's and approached the hostess stand that was just inside of the front door, smiling at Celeste, the hostess.

"Hiya Mac, table for two?" Celeste asked.

"If you have one," Mac replied. Russo's always kept a few tables open for select customers, and Mac, Emma and Mads had been placed on that list since moving in above the popular location. Between the three of them they visited it almost daily, the owner gave them a discount on their meals, and it was a relaxed and welcoming atmosphere.

"Of course we do," Celeste said, as a few customers who were waiting to be seated groaned in disapproval at Mac being pushed ahead of them. "Your favorite table is open."

"Thanks Celeste," Mac said as she walked straight ahead, through the bar area, nodding hello to the bartenders and servers as she made her way to the row of high-top tables that ran along the window, sitting down at the second to last one.

"Hi."

She jumped a bit as the words were whispered in her ear, then smiled.

"Sorry to scare you, I came in through the back door. Perks of the job."

Mac's stomach did a flip as Rigsy kissed her before sitting down at the table. Even though they saw each other almost every day she still felt butterflies. Of course, it was possible that it was because they didn't get to spend a lot of time together. Rigsy worked long shifts on the police force, and summer was the busiest season and meant lots of overtime. Mac tried not to complain about the lack of time that they spent together, focusing more on making the time they did get together as special as possible. Besides, as soon as Labor Day passed by, and the crowds left, Rigsy wouldn't have all of the overtime or be needed seven days a week.

"My favorite couple!," Sam, the waitress, gushed as she placed two coasters down on the table. "What can I get you guys?"

"You decide," Mac told Rigsy.

"Firecracker nachos with crispy wontons, pulled chicken, cheese and spicy sour cream," Rigsy said, as the two women laughed.

"Officer Riggs, you know the menu better than I do," Sam joked. "What about drinks?"

"I'll take a vodka cranberry with lemon please," Mac said.

"I'll take a Jameson on the rocks," Rigsy added.

"Whiskey on the rocks? That's aggressive. Did you have a bad day?" Mac asked after Sam left.

"No, the opposite, actually," Rigsy answered, grinning. "I was asked if I would be interested in working for the state."

"The state? Really?"

"The State Police. They have an academy soon, and the Chief approved me leaving to take it. He's the one who brought it up to me, actually."

"Rigsy! That's awesome! I'm so proud of you."

The State Police were known as the best of the best when it came to law enforcement in Maine. Rigsy had mentioned in the past about wanting to be a State Trooper, but he'd been hesitant to pursue it as he didn't want to upset his boss, the Chief of Police. Mac could picture how handsome he'd be in the dark blue uniform, complete with knee high black shiny boots and the hat. Given the fact that he was well over six feet tall his size fit right along with the perception of the State Police, they were larger than life, or at least it seemed that way when you saw them standing on the side of the highway.

"It's kind of last minute, that's the only negative," he said, making room on their table as Sam set their drinks and appetizer down.

"Huh?"

"The notice. The academy starts a week from today, and it's four weeks long."

"Oh. Where is it?" Mac asked.

"It's in Vassalaboro," Rigsy said, reaching out and taking Mac's hand in his. "Don't freak out."

"I'm not going to freak out," Mac lied. Vassalaboro was two hours away from Summer Cove. "That's a long commute, though."

"It would be if I was driving back and forth every day, but we sleep over. We're there for the whole four weeks."

Mac's heart sank as she watched him place a pile of the nachos on a plate for her, spooning some of the spicy sour cream onto the side of her plate like she preferred.

"Hold on. You're going away for a month?" she asked him, reaching for her drink.

"Now you know why I said don't freak out. I'll still have my phone, don't worry. We can still talk every day."

"I know, but it just stinks that you're leaving, summer will be over when you come back," Mac said softly as she picked at her nachos. She didn't want to make him feel bad for leaving, this was a terrific opportunity for him. But she'd gotten used to seeing him every day, even if it was just driving by where he was directing traffic to say a quick hello. Not seeing him for an entire month hadn't been something that she'd foreseen happening. "I'm happy for you though, really."

"It will go by fast, I promise. Besides, you have that new client you'll be working with anyway, right? The Van Rohrer's? That will probably eat up all of your time."

"Hopefully," Mac said. "I still have to write up the proposal and present it to them. If I land it, I really think it could be big for my business, to bring in more clients I mean."

Things hadn't gone as well as Mac had assumed they would with her new business endeavor. She'd done a great job with her parent's store and started work at the Sandy Shore Resort almost immediately after, but so far that'd been it. She had worked at the resort on several projects over the last few months and enjoyed it, but she had realized that jobs don't just fall into your lap. She needed to be proactive and walk into businesses and sell herself, and that was much easier said than done. If she landed the job with the Van Rhorer's it would be huge for her, everyone knew the store name so well.

"So, it isn't just me who has good news about work then," he said, raising his glass to her. "Cheers to the two of us, moving up that corporate ladder. Uh, kind of."

Mac laughed as she lightly tapped her glass against his.

She hoped that he was right, right about both things actually. That she'd get the job for the Van Rohrer's, and that the four weeks he was gone would fly by.

CHAPTER FOUR

"I saw that, Rose," Mac said to the feisty hen, quickly lifting her leg up before Rose pecked at her ankle.

She hadn't slept much the night before and had found herself wide awake at five that morning and decided she may as well go to her parent's house and collect the eggs for her mom. Since moving into the apartment, she hadn't done it much, and she found it oddly therapeutic, aside from dodging Rose.

"Well, you're up early," Mac's mom said as she stood in the barn doorway. "Is everything okay?"

"It's fine. I was wide awake and antsy, I thought I'd come by and bug Rose," Mac joked as she finished collecting the eggs.

"Will you stay for breakfast?" her mother asked, as Muckie came flying around the corner of the barn. "I just put some bacon on."

"Sure," Mac said, patting Muckie as he bumped up against her legs before making her way to the house.

As soon as she stepped inside she could smell the maple bacon that was on the stove, and the fresh coffee brewing in the ancient Mr. Coffee that her parents had. She'd tried to talk them into getting a Keurig, explaining that it would be easier for them, but they'd both looked at her like she was crazy.

"Hi dad," she said as she took a coffee mug out of the cabinet.

"Well, you're here awfully early. Are you okay?" he asked her as he sat down and started to put his sneakers on.

"I couldn't sleep, so I thought I'd hang out with Rose for a bit," Mac joked, stirring her coffee as she sat down.

"Better you than me, I can't move fast enough to get out of her way these days," her father said, chuckling. "I'm going to go for my walk. Try and save me some bacon, would you?"

Mac smiled as she watched him leave, Muckie alongside him, wagging his tail excitedly.

"It's good that he's still doing his exercises, but he's moving kind of slow," Mac said as she watched her mother flip the bacon, her stomach growling in anticipation.

"Yes, he's been incredibly good with the exercises, walking every morning. He still gets stiff, though. Mornings are bad, that's why he's moving slow. That hip will never be the same," her mother said as she placed a heap of bacon on Mac's plate, along with two fried eggs. "How did that meeting go? The one with the Van Rohrer's? Was their house as fancy as I'd guessed that it would be?"

"Yup," Mac said in between bites of bacon. "I only saw the foyer and their office, but the house is a mansion, just like you predicted. They have a long driveway that leads to the house, and it's a circle at the end of the driveway with a big fountain in the middle of it."

"A fountain," Mac's mom said, sitting down. "I wonder how well that works in the wintertime around here."

"It's probably heated, they've got the money to spend. Anyway, the meeting went well, I'm writing up my proposal for them today. I really want the job, I hope I get it."

"I'm sure you will. You've done a wonderful job so far, with the store and then the Sandy Shore. That new reservation system is all that Barbara talks about."

"I'm glad they like it. Mads hates it, but that's probably because she'd rather be working with Rylan anyway," Mac joked.

"Oh, I'm sure," her mom laughed. "And how is Rigsy? I've been busy with customers when he's come by the store for his daily dose of caffeine."

"He's good. Too good, actually. The Chief approved for him to go attend the State Police Academy up in Vassalaboro."

"Oh Mac! That's wonderful!"

"Yeah, except it means that he's gone for a month," Mac groaned.

"Well, that's what comes with the territory, I suppose. His training that he already took can't somehow be transferred? Like a credit in school?"

"I guess not," Mac answered, shrugging. "I'm just mad that he's leaving. Well, not mad. Sad is what I mean, I guess. I hadn't planned on my boyfriend being gone for the rest of the summer."

"Well, maybe this will cheer you up. Or not," her mother said, standing up and taking an envelope out of the mail pile and placing it next to Mac's plate.

"What's this?" Mac asked as she stared at the envelope, the return address sticking out to her like a sore thumb.

"Mackenzie, how would I know? I didn't open it up."

Mac finished eating her eggs, staring at the envelope as her mother cleaned the dishes.

"Are you going to stare at it or open it up?" her mother asked her as she dried her hands on a dish towel.

"Stare at it," Mac replied, standing up to wash off her plate.

"Should I have thrown it away? Because I did consider doing that, you know. But it's not my place to."

"No. It's not a big deal, it's probably something really dumb," Mac replied as she put her dish in the dishwasher and turned around slowly, looking at the envelope. "I need to get some stuff from my room."

She grabbed the envelope off of the table and trotted off upstairs to her bedroom, knowing full well that her mother knew it was just an excuse for her to open the letter alone. She flopped down on her bed, her eyes focusing on the upper left of the envelope.

Austin DeLong

Mac hadn't talked to Austin since his call after she'd walked out on him and his parents, and a short while later she'd blocked him on her phone as well as on all social media. He hadn't necessarily done anything to warrant being blocked, she just didn't want to come across his face on her Instagram feed or be tempted to text him. Not that she would. She was perfectly content with Rigsy.

She opened the envelope and pulled out the piece of paper that was folded inside, unfolding it slowly as if something might jump out at her.

Mackenzie,

I've tried calling you and messaging you for months. I guess you don't want to speak to me, and I can understand why. I shouldn't have made the assumptions that I did about your life after we graduated, that you would want to stay at home instead of starting your career. I didn't treat you with respect at the dinner with my parents, and I regret it every day.

Life here isn't the same without you. No one can ever take your place. You are beautiful, smart, and funny, and I need you back in my life. I think about you every day, about us every day.

I miss my best friend and girlfriend. We spent four years together and it was the best time of my life, don't you feel the same?

Please forgive me for what I said and come back to our home.

Love,

Austin

Mac stared at the letter and started to wad it into a ball, then reconsidered and opened it back up, smoothing it out on her bed.

Four years was a long time to be with someone and then just abruptly cut them out of your life. She would be lying to herself if she said she hadn't thought about Austin since the breakup. She had done it so fast, breaking up with him, walking out of his life and literally flying across the country, never returning to him again. There wasn't any closure that way, and she didn't know why, but lately she'd felt that she needed it. Why had he assumed that she would want to stay home when they had talked about her hopes of getting a job after graduation? Why hadn't he talked to her about it, and if he was okay with her working then why didn't he say so at that dinner with his parents? She wanted answers, and she hated that she didn't know why she suddenly felt the urge to talk to him and get them because overall it didn't even matter.

She reached for her phone, hesitating, and then quickly tapped on his name and unblocked him. She wasn't going to initiate any contact with him, but if he reached out to her she might reply.

"Mac?"

"Coming, mom!" Mac yelled, grabbing the letter, and folding it up and then placing it back in the envelope. She tossed it on top of her nightstand before leaving the room.

"Is everything okay?" her mother asked, raising an eyebrow as Mac walked past her.

"Yup, everything's fine," Mac answered. "I should head home and get started on the proposal for the Van Rohrer's, it's going to take me a good ten hours, maybe even more. Thanks for breakfast."

She hurried out the door to her car, feeling like she'd just committed a crime by unblocking Austin, which was ridiculous. It wasn't a big deal at all.

CHAPTER FIVE

"This is very thorough."

Mac looked across the table at Mr. Van Rohrer as he read her proposal, pausing to bite into his Caprese salad.

They were eating lunch outside on the back patio at the Van Rohrer's house, which was an extremely impressive space. The back patio had a full kitchen, complete with a brick pizza oven and rotisserie, the latter of which lunch had been cooked on, a crisp and moist rotisserie chicken.

"It sure is eye opening," Mrs. Van Rohrer said, dabbing at the corner of her mouth with a linen napkin. Mac couldn't help but notice that the napkin had Mrs. Van Rohrer's pink lipstick on it, and she wondered how many napkins had to be washed every week.

"I try to cover everything in my proposals," Mac said, smiling at Bernie, one of the Van Rohrer's employees, as he refilled her water glass. She'd spent much longer on it then she'd thought she would. It had taken her a few days, working twelve hours a day between researching and writing it up. Had she been too inclusive? Maybe they didn't need to know as much as she had outlined. This was only the second time that she'd written a proposal up, and the one she had done for Mad's parents hadn't been nearly as detailed as this one was.

"It's disappointing," Mr. Van Rohrer said, shutting the proposal and holding his glass up for Bernie to fill with more water.

"I'm sorry, what part?" Mac asked, confused. She wasn't sure what would be disappointing, she'd spent so much time on it.

"The whole thing," he sighed, leaning back in his chair. "I knew this would happen."

"Oh, stop being dramatic, Bob," Mrs. Van Rohrer said, looking at Mac. "It's not your proposal that is disappointing, it's that the General Manager clearly isn't doing their job."

"Oh. Well, that can be fixed. I'm happy to work with her to implement these changes," Mac said enthusiastically.

"It's a him. And he's been known to be stubborn," Mr. Van Rohrer said, running his hands through his short salt and pepper colored hair.

"I can work with stubborn," Mac joked uneasily. She wasn't sure that she could, of course, but she really needed this job.

"The potential increase in revenue is higher than I thought it would be," Mrs. Van Rohrer said, steering the conversation away from the General Manager. "How did you come up with these numbers?"

"I researched the top three competitors you have in this area, looked at their numbers compared to yours, plugged in estimates in the areas that I've targeted, and the result was these numbers."

"But we have to pay a pretty penny for new inventory," Mr. Van Rohrer mumbled.

"Yes, but to be blunt your existing inventory on many things is far too outdated, and that's why they aren't selling," Mac explained.

"It's well-known brands," he told her, holding up a chicken leg. "In fact, I picked out a lot of the men's clothing."

"Yes, it's brands that an older demographic would purchase," Mac said, not wanting to offend him. "Your target demographic is the twenty-five to thirty-five age range. They grew up with their parents buying those brands. An example is Jordache. Super popular in the seventies and eighties, not so much now. Abercrombie, Hollister, Good American if you can offer those brands they'd fly off the rack. Same goes with vintage items, Levi's as an example, and old concert T-shirts like the Rolling Stones or Nirvana. You aren't making any money with the same clothes sitting in inventory for months," Mac explained. "On the other side, if you turn to page six, you do well with a lot of the existing home goods that you sell. All I suggest changing with that department is the layout, organizing it more so things are easier to find and see, which will translate into more sales."

"You mentioned the floor needing to be replaced. That seems like a royal pain in the butt," Mrs. Van Rohrer said, frowning. "I don't want to close the store at all."

"Not entirely replaced. The areas where the floor is lifting up need to be fixed, it looks terrible. If patches aren't too obvious then that's what I suggest going with. The work can be done after hours and is fairly easy, I spoke with the contractor that could do it." Mac left out the part about the contractor being Gus the floor guy, a regular from Russo's bar, she had run down to ask him questions at midnight as she was finishing the proposal. Her heart sank as she realized that she'd gone overboard with the proposal, and mild panic started to sink in as she thought about where she would get her next customer from.

The Van Rohrer's looked at each other and Mac bit her lip nervously, pushing the heirloom tomato around on her plate before Mrs. Van Rohrer spoke.

"Mackenzie, how soon can you start?"

***

The light from the full moon lit up the boats in the cove, the slight rocking in the water creating hypnotic ripples. Mac sighed as she played with the starfish charm on her bangle bracelet that Rigsy had given her earlier on their date. They'd gone to dinner at the Lobster Barn, which by pure luck had a table available without a reservation. Dinner had been baked stuffed lobster and the owner, Chad, had sent over tiramisu for dessert. He'd said it was on the house, in celebration of Rigsy leaving to go to the State Police Academy. It seemed everyone in town knew that Rigsy was leaving, which wasn't exactly surprising. All the locals knew him.

"I hate that you're leaving," she said, putting her head on his shoulder.

"Me too," he replied, kissing the top of her head.

"Summer will be over by the time you're done."

"Yup, and you'll be spending your first winter in Summer Cove in four years, and I absolutely look forward to torturing you with the snow," Rigsy teased, tousling her hair as he turned to look at her, his head moving to the left. "Did you see that?"

He sat up straight, then slid off of the rock that they were sitting on as he looked over towards the area where Mac's apartment was.

"See what?" Mac asked, taking his hand as she slid down the rock and stood next to him.

She squinted her eyes and saw a figure standing in front of Russo's front door. It was past closing time, and while the staff stayed later to clean up and sometimes hang out the lights were all off inside the bar.

"Stay here," Rigsy told her in a stern voice.

"What? No!" she whispered loudly as she followed behind him, the two of them crouched over a bit trying to remain hidden behind the large rocks.

The figure walked over towards the alleyway that led to Mac's apartment and her heart started to race. She wasn't sure about Mads whereabouts, but she knew that Emma was home alone.

As if he could read her mind, Rigsy let go of her hand and sprinted towards the figure. "Hey!"

Mac's heart raced, worried that whoever the person was might have a knife or a gun and hurt Rigsy. She watched as the figure looked at Rigsy running towards them in the semi-dark parking lot. The person started to run, and Mac shrieked as she watched Rigsy catch up to them and lunge, grabbing the person's legs and taking them down to the ground. She ran across the parking lot towards them, simultaneously fumbling around in her purse for her phone so she could call the police.

"Get off of me!"

Mac heard the familiar voice as she caught up to Rigsy, who was now standing up, brushing himself off.

"What are you doing here?" Rigsy asked, holding his hand out to help the person up.

"Mark?" Mac asked, bewildered. "Why are you creeping around my apartment at two in the morning?"

"I wasn't creeping, I was leaving," Mark said, rubbing his neck. "I saw you two and turned around to run back inside but it was too late."

Mac's jaw dropped in shock as she looked at Rigsy.

"Leaving where?" Rigsy asked Mark.

"Leaving the apartment. Emma. I was with Emma."

"Oh my God, what did you do to her?" Mac demanded.

"Huh?" Mark asked, shaking the gravel off of his jeans.

"Uh, Mac, I don't think he did anything to her. Well, anything bad, I mean," Rigsy said, raising his eyebrows as he spoke.

"I'm so confused right now," Mac said.

"Mark and I have been seeing each other."

Mac turned around to look at Emma, standing there in her big white fuzzy slippers, her hair haphazardly piled on top of her head, wearing a pair of short flannel shorts and a red cropped tank top.

Mac didn't know what to say, she was too shocked at what Emma had just said.

"I thought you were a burglar or something," Rigsy explained. "Sorry, man."

"It's fine, seeing a man outside of your girl's place at this hour I understand being concerned. For obvious reasons I haven't been over here at normal times," Mark explained.

"Hold on. You've been to our place more than once?" Mac asked, looking over at Emma, who had kept this secret for God knows how long.

"Guys, it's late, and I'm standing here in my pajamas. We should go inside," Emma said.

"I should be getting home, my car's over there," Mark said, pointing down the road. He kissed Emma goodbye and walked away briskly, leaving Mac, Emma and Rigsy standing in silence in the middle of the parking lot.

"Well, I should probably head home too. I leave in a few hours," Rigsy said to Mac. "I'd sleep over, but I have a feeling you and Emma have some stuff to catch up on. I'll swing by in the morning before I leave, okay?"

"Okay," Mac reluctantly agreed, hugging him, and giving him a kiss before he left.

"You have a lot of explaining to do," she said to Emma, annoyed that this had interrupted her last night with Rigsy before he left for the academy.

"I know," Emma sighed. "Let's go get it over with."

The two walked back to the apartment, where Mac grabbed each of them a wine cooler from the fridge before they settled onto the couch.

"Okay, I'm all ears," she said to Emma, taking a sip of her drink, questioning how Emma could even think about hooking up with Mark after what he had done to her.

"It started around a month ago. He came into the store, and for whatever reason we had an actual adult conversation, you know, instead of me just ignoring him like I had been. Just light and fluffy, it wasn't anything scandalous. And then later that night I texted him."

"What? *YOU* texted *HIM*?" Mac asked, bewildered. She had assumed that if anyone had instigated this it was Mark, not Emma.

"Yeah," Emma shrugged. "It came out of nowhere really. I didn't plan it. The band downstairs was on break and that lady who sings karaoke decided to belt out that song from the movie A Star is Born, and that brought back memories, and I texted him some dumb line about the movie, and things just went from there."

"Emma, this guy was your husband and he cheated on you. And he tried to stop my parents store from expanding. Please make this make sense to me, why you're hooking up with him? There are tons of eligible men around here to hook up with."

"It's more than just hooking up, Mac."

"Oh, come on! Emma!" Mac couldn't believe what she was hearing. "What about Tracy?"

"They broke up, everyone knows that."

"Right, except you just said this has been going on for a month which is also when they called off their engagement. Let me guess, it's just a coincidence, right?"

"Honestly? Yes. They'd already called off the engagement."

Mac rolled her eyes in disbelief.

"And that eye roll is why we've kept it a secret. Or tried to, anyway. We knew everyone would assume that he ended the engagement because of me, that he was cheating on Tracy with me," Emma said.

"Can you blame people for assuming that? So, what was your plan, to just sneak around and hide it for however long it lasts?" Mac asked.

"Of course not. It isn't like this was planned, Mac. I hated him six months ago, I didn't ever think that would ever change."

"Then why did it? Change, I mean. Your feelings, what made you change? How can you ever trust him again, Emma?"

"He said it was the biggest mistake of his life, that he will regret it forever. The pressure from his parents was too much for him, it always has been."

"So, his parents made him cheat on you?" Mac asked sarcastically.

"You know how much his parents didn't want him to marry me," Emma said, tears in her eyes. "Do you know how hurtful it was for me? They've known me my entire life, but I've never been good enough for their son. Ever. Not when we were little kids and not now when we are adults. Do you have any idea how humiliated I was when we got married, that Mad's parents had to pay for everything, because Mark's parents hated me so much they refused to acknowledge the wedding? They were terrible to him over it, always telling him he could do better than me. How could he not eventually break down and believe them?"

"Because he loved you, that's how," Mac replied firmly.

"When I was out on dates with other guys I still thought about Mark. I couldn't help it, I tried not to, but no matter who I was with I eventually thought about Mark. He's cut off his parents now, he doesn't talk to them anymore because of me."

"Maybe he should have done that years ago, Em. Why didn't he? Cut them off, I mean."

"He needed their help financially. Who do you think paid for the place in New York? They helped out at first, but then started to have strings attached when I moved there. Mac, we can't change the past. I know you're just trying to look out for me, and you have to understand I wouldn't just jump back into a relationship with him if I didn't know that it would be different now. And it has been. I'm so happy with him, and he is with me, too. And that's all that matters, isn't it? That I'm happy?"

Mac suddenly realized why Emma looked so good over the last few weeks, it was because of Mark. Mac couldn't argue with that, she just hoped that this time it would last.

CHAPTER SIX

Mac felt a hand on her shoulder and rolled over in bed slowly, smiling as she saw Rigsy.

"Sorry to wake you up," he whispered, holding up a coffee. "It might be too early for you, but I grabbed you one while I was there. I need the caffeine for the ride and I'm guessing you were up late with Emma."

"You're right. I still can't believe she's back with Mark," Mac said as she sat up and took the coffee from him, taking a sip of it before placing it down on her nightstand. She swung her legs over the side of the bed and reached out to hug him.

"I'm going to miss you," she said.

"I'll miss you, too. I'll be back before you know it, and I'll call you as soon as I can."

Mac held onto him, not wanting to let go.

"Okay. Text me when you get there so I know that you made it safe," she said, backing up to kiss him.

"I will."

She hugged him one more time before walking him out to the door, kissing him again before he left. She hurried out to the deck to wave goodbye to him, watching as he drove out of the cove.

She closed her eyes, listening to the sound of the seagulls crying as they scoured the parking lot in the cove for remnants of food from the night before, a stray French fry that someone dropped or a piece of a hamburger bun. The fishing boats in the cove started to come alive, the fishermen climbing aboard the wooden boats and talking to each other loudly, laughing as they got the traps ready for the day.

Sitting down she watched the sun rise off in the horizon, looking as if it came straight out of the ocean as it slowly rose into the sky. She inhaled deeply and closed her eyes, thinking about how lucky she was to live right on the ocean.

"Hey!"

Mac sat up, startled. She'd fallen asleep on the deck to the sound of the waves and Mads was now hovering over her as she threw Cheerios to Sammy the seagull.

"What time is it?" Mac asked.

"Eight. Did you sleep out here or something?" Mads asked.

"No. Rigsy came over at five to say goodbye and I came out here after he left."

"He didn't sleep over?" Mads asked, dragging a chair over to sit next to Mac.

"No. There was an incident. Kind of."

"Incident? What kind of incident?" Mads asked, waving to one of the fishermen.

Mac craned her neck, looking around the corner of the deck towards the slider.

"Emma's back with Mark," she whispered to Mads.

"WHAT?" Mads barked.

"SHH! Emma's here you dummy!"

"Well how did you expect me to react to that news?" Mads asked as she sat down. "You can't be serious. Are you sure?"

"Yes, I'm sure. Last night after we went out to eat Rigsy and I sat over there on the rocks to hang out and talk, and after we'd been there for a while he saw someone outside of Russo's. It was past closing time, we thought it was someone trying to break into the apartment, and long story short it was Mark."

"Did Rigsy beat him up?" Mads asked.

"What? No. He did tackle him, though. I wish I had it on video, it looked cool. Anyway, Emma came out and explained that they've been seeing each other for a while now."

"I don't believe it," Mads said, shaking her head in disbelief.

"Believe what?" Emma asked.

"That you're back together with your dufus ex-husband," Mads said to Emma.

"So much for keeping it a secret," Emma said to Mads, looking over at Mac. "Thanks a lot, Mac."

Mac stood up and followed Emma into their apartment, with Mads right behind her.

"Em, it isn't like Mads wouldn't have found out," Mac said. She hadn't known that Emma didn't want Mads to know, anyway.

"Why is it a secret?" Mads asked.

"Because we don't want to have to answer all of the stupid questions people ask," Emma said angrily, walking to her bedroom and slamming the door shut.

"This is when sharing a room with her stinks," Mads said, sighing. "There's no way I'm going in there to get my clothes."

"She'll get over it," Mac said, sighing heavily as she started to toast herself a bagel. "I'm sure you have clothes at the resort."

"What's that supposed to mean?"

"Umm, just that you stay there more often than not, so it's probably accurate that there's a pile of your clothes in Rylan's room?" Mac reached for the ibuprofen, she could feel a headache starting.

"I don't have any clothes there."

"What's the big deal? Why does it matter that you're seeing Rylan, Mads? We all know him now, we all like him. It's okay if you actually have a long-term relationship with one of the guys you meet over the summer, you know."

"Maybe he doesn't want one with me, have you thought of that?"

Mac paused before spreading a thick layer of cream cheese on her bagel. "No, I haven't. You're telling me Rylan doesn't want a long-term thing with you?"

Mads shrugged as she stuffed a bagel into the toaster.

"I don't believe it. He seems so into you, and you two have been glued to the hip almost all summer. I think you're simply scared to put your feelings out there," Mac said as she sat down on the sofa. "Face it, you've never dated anyone longer than for a summer."

"You're right, I haven't. So what?"

"So maybe it's time you let yourself have feelings for someone for a change, serious ones I mean," Mac suggested.

Mads rolled her eyes as she placed a hunk of butter on her bagel. "Okay mom."

The bedroom door opened, and Emma walked into the bathroom, not saying a word to either girl. Mads dropped the bagel onto her plate and ran into the bedroom, appearing a few minutes later with a pile of clothes that she dropped on the couch.

"As soon as I'm done eating I'll change and then we should get to the resort so we can finish having Rylan hang stuff in the lobby," Mads said.

Mac nodded her head in agreement and went to her room to change, not daring to ask Emma how long she'd be in the bathroom so she could take a quick shower. She'd give Emma some time to cool off.

CHAPTER SEVEN

"Here?"

"A little more to the right," Mac said, squinting her eyes. "Perfect."

"He sure is," Mads whispered, making Mac laugh.

"Thanks Rylan, it looks good."

"No problem Mac," Rylan replied, grinning at she and Mads. "I'll go grab the paint and get started on the last room."

Mac and Mads stood in silence in the resorts lobby, watching Rylan walk away.

"I hate to see him leave, but I love to watch him go," Mads joked.

"He's definitely one good looking guy, that's for sure," Mac said. "You really need to tell him."

"Tell him what?" Mads asked, wiping a smudge off of one of the lobby mirrors.

"That you'd like to keep seeing him after he's done here this summer."

Mads frowned at Mac.

"Well, since he's almost done with his job here you might want to think about it before he leaves. Just saying," Mac said.

"Yeah, yeah. Easier said than done. Maybe I should just text him some song lyrics or whatever it was that Emma did to woo Mark back," Mads joked.

"Maybe. It sure did work for her, she and Mark practically have hearts floating over their heads they're so lovey dovey," Mac said, causing Mads to laugh and roll her eyes.

"I still can't believe they are back together," Mads said.

"I KNEW IT!"

Mac and Mads both spun around to face Tracy, who was standing in front of the salon space in the lobby, hands on her hips.

"I knew he got back together with her!" Tracy said loudly.

Mac didn't know what to say and looked over at Mads, who seemed to be just as surprised as Mac was.

"Are you spying on us?" Mads asked Tracy. "First of all, the last I heard you and Mark broke up. And second, hanging around, lurking to eavesdrop on us is creepy."

"Oh please. I'm not spying, I'm getting my salon ready to open. You two talk so loud it's impossible not to hear you. And as far as what you heard about Mark and I breaking up, did you also hear that we broke up because of your friend?"

"Don't blame Emma for breaking up your relationship, you did it on your own," Mac said.

"Really? Then why has it been some big secret about them getting back together? Why would they hide it, sneaking around town and trying not to be seen?"

Mac hated to admit that Tracy had a good point.

"Probably because Emma knew everyone would think she was a fool for taking him back after what he did to her, that's why. And it isn't a secret, obviously, if it was then we wouldn't know," Mads said confidently.

"Yeah? Well then, since it wasn't a secret, maybe I should tell the secret that I know. You know, since everyone's being so truthful and all now," Tracy smugly replied.

"Tracy, I don't care about your secret, and I doubt anyone else does, either" Mads said to her.

"Oh, I bet Mark would care," Tracy replied, smiling. "You'd all care, because after all, you were there."

Mac and Mads watched as Tracy turned and walked back into her salon, her long blonde hair swaying back and forth with each step that she took.

Mac turned to Mads, her heart racing a bit.

"Are you thinking what I am?"

****

Mac and Mads entered Walsh's Market on Maine and made a beeline towards Emma, who was behind the counter counting muffins.

"We have an issue," Mads said to Emma.

"Huh?" Emma looked up at Mads and then at Mac. "What kind of issue? What's going on?"

"I'll take one of those lemon poppy seed muffins please. They're so big I'm splitting one with my husband."

Mac and Mads stepped aside as Emma gave the customer what she asked for, the line of customers growing behind the counter.

"How long is the wait for a smoothie?" someone asked.

"Can we go talk somewhere private?" Mads asked, agitated. "This place is swamped."

"Mike, can you help this gentleman out?" Emma asked one of the other employees, as she stepped out from behind the counter. "I'll be back in a few minutes."

"Let's go out back," Mac suggested, leading them through the store and out the back door.

"Okay, what's going on? I'm super busy right now," Emma said.

"Tracy knows," Mads said.

"Tracy knows what?" Emma asked, rolling her eyes.

"She knows that you and Mark are back together, and she knows about what happened with the guard stand years ago. She said she's going to tell," Mac explained.

The golden tan on Emma's face turned pale white as she looked back and forth between Mac and Mads.

"How? How did she find out?" Emma asked.

Mac and Mads looked at each other, neither one saying a word.

"Well?" Emma asked again, firmly.

"We were in the lobby at the Sandy Shore talking and Tracy overheard us. We had no idea that she was even there, her salon isn't open yet. I'm sorry, Mads," Mac said softly.

"We were just joking around, Mac asked me about Rylan, and I made a comparison about you and Mark. I'm sorry, too," Mads added.

Emma sighed heavily, flipping over a plastic milk crate with her foot and sitting down on it. "Well, I guess she was going to find out sooner or later."

"She said that you're the reason Mark called off the engagement, that's why she's so mad. She said you were trying to keep it a secret, and then she said something about a secret, that she was going to tell a secret that we had all been there for," Mads explained. "She's got to be talking about the guard stand, right?"

"There's no way that she would know about that night. She wasn't there," Emma said confidently, shaking her head no.

"Then what else could she be talking about?" Mac asked.

"Maybe she's just talking nonsense, trying to cause drama," Mads said. "She is kind of a drama queen, after all."

"Emma, do you think Mark told her? When they were together, I mean," Mac asked.

"I don't see why he would. It isn't like that would come up in conversation, right? It isn't like it's cool or anything. Besides, we all made a promise never to tell."

"I know, but sometimes you tell your significant other things that are a secret, you know? Maybe it came up somehow when they were engaged," Mac said.

"I guess it could have," Emma said, tapping her foot nervously.

Mac bit her lip as her mind raced. If Tracy did know about what had happened and told the police it would spread through the town like wildfire. It would affect all of them, regardless of the fact it had happened a few years ago.

"Well, we need to find out what she's talking about, and nip this in the bud. Do you remember what a big deal it was for the town to have to pay for the repairs, and how hard they tried to find out who did it? We will all look like total jerks if it comes out that we were there and never told anyone," Mads said as she paced back and forth. "My parents will kill me."

"Mark could lose his job," Emma said. "Mac, it isn't good for you guys, either."

Mac looked at Emma and nodded her head in agreement. "I know, hopefully the Van Rohrer's wouldn't take it into consideration."

"Well, yeah, there's that but what about Rigsy?" Mads asked.

"What about him?" Mac asked, confused. Rigsy was all set with his job.

"Mac, if the State Police find out that he left the scene of an accident and then lied to the police about being there do you think they'd still want to hire him?" Mads asked. "You know how things are today. Everyone wants total accountability."

Mac's heart sunk, she hadn't thought about that at all.

"This isn't good for any of us," Mac said nervously, biting the inside of her cheek. She wasn't sure what she could do, but she needed to do something.

****

"How could you two be so stupid?"

"Excuse me?" Mac asked angrily.

"You know what I mean. Talking about Emma and Mark right in front of Tracy's salon. Of course she would hear what you were saying. Why are you gossiping about this, anyway? Do you realize what could happen to me, Mac?"

Mac sighed heavily and rolled over on her bed. This was the first call that she'd had from Rigsy since he had gone to the academy, and it hadn't gone as she had expected. Instead of a conversation filled with "I miss you," and "I can't wait to get back," she'd had to listen to him explain all of the things he was doing, and how nice it was in that area, and how he had been asked about getting involved with forensics. He'd also explained that he couldn't use his phone at all during the day, and that it was frowned upon to use it at all. Now she'd told him what Tracy had said and he was mad.

"You're not the only person that could be in trouble, Rigsy. Mark's an attorney now, remember? And don't call me stupid again, either. I obviously wouldn't do this on purpose."

"Sorry, I shouldn't have called you stupid. I just don't need to worry about this, have it hanging over my head. I know Mark doesn't either, none of us do."

"Don't worry about it, she's probably bluffing anyway," Mac lied. "By the way, it isn't like I'd want the Van Rohrer's asking me about it if the news got out, you know."

"I know, I know. Just make sure you don't do anything else to antagonize her, okay?" Rigsy asked.

"Uh, sure. I don't know why you're acting like I'm the bad guy in this," Mac said. She knew that he would be upset about it but hadn't thought he would actually be mad at her, she assumed he'd be upset with Tracy like everyone else was.

"Alright, let's change the topic. How's things with the Van Rohrer's?" he asked.

"Well, the General Manager blew me off twice so far to do the store walk through, so I guess you could say things aren't going great. Luckily it's been great beach weather, so at least I've been able to get some beach time in."

"Hmm. Well, I'm sure you'll get them in shape."

"I'm trying but what am I supposed to do? Go there and start without him?" Mac asked. She was frustrated with the situation. She could do a lot of the inventory work from home on her laptop, but the rest required her to be onsite.

"Why not? They hired you to do a job, right? He's already wasted almost a week. What happens if you just show up and start without him?"

"I don't know," Mac groaned. She didn't want to talk about work. Calling the Van Rohrer's and telling them that their General Manager had cancelled the meetings she had with him wasn't something she wanted to do, it made her look bad, but she didn't know how to force someone to show up for a meeting.

"You'll get back on track," Rigsy said reassuringly.

"What's that mean? When did I fall off?" Mac asked.

"I just meant that you've spent a lot of the summer hanging out at the beach, and at Russo's. You haven't exactly been out looking for new customers, Mac. You were handed the resort job. You need to be assertive now on this job."

"Well, that was blunt," Mac said, unsure if she should be upset or not. "You know, it hasn't.."

"I have to go," Rigsy interrupted her mid-sentence. "I'm sorry, I'll text or call you when I can."

Mac looked at the phone and then put it down next to her. Even though what Rigsy had said was hard to hear he was right. The work she had done at the resort wasn't full time, and she had intended on getting another customer to work with at the same time. But summer had kicked in, and she hadn't been to the beach in so long that she found herself spending mornings at the resort and then lounging on the beach for a few hours during the day, since she was already there. And after coming home from the beach a quick shower and meeting friends for some food and drinks at Russo's was the perfect way to end the day. With her rent so low she didn't worry much about paying her bills, but she also wasn't saving a lot of money and she knew she should be. She'd been coasting and had taken it easy so far, she knew she had.

She reached for her phone and texted Blaize, the General Manager, telling him when she was going to the store. She wasn't asking, she was telling, and if he wasn't there then she would start without him.

CHAPTER EIGHT

Mac looked at her phone to check the time, then stood up to stretch. She'd been at the Van Rohrer's store waiting to meet Blaize, the General Manager, for over half an hour. When she'd been told what his name was she'd assumed he would be trouble, with a name like Blaize, spelt with a Z, how could he not? She'd had to wait in the employee break room for him, which was a small room with three small round tables, uncomfortable metal chairs, a few vending machines, and an old yellow refrigerator. It smelled stale in the room, like someone had left food in the refrigerator for too long or the trash hadn't been emptied in a while. Just as she stood up to go wait outside the door opened.

The man who had entered was the same one that she had seen when she'd been evaluating the store, the one who had been flirting with one of the employees.

"Mackenzie?" he asked as he walked towards one of the vending machines.

"Yes. Are you Blaize?" she asked him, watching as he fed two one-dollar bills into the soda machine.

"Yep, that's me," he answered, popping open the top on the can of Coke he had and chugging the whole thing down, squashing the can in his hands when he was done.

"I'm Mac," she said, extending her hand towards him.

"No kidding," he replied smugly as he threw the can into the trash barrel across the room. "I thought maybe you were a new employee that I forgot I'd hired."

Mac picked up her notepad, flipping it open. She wasn't sure why he was being so sarcastic to her, or not apologizing for being late, but she was there to do a job whether he liked it or not. She wasn't in any mood for his attitude, she was tired, having stayed up until midnight the night before waiting for Rigsy to call or text her, which he hadn't. Then she'd started to worry about Tracy again.

"Well, I'd hope that if I was a new employee you'd at least be on time for my first day of work," she said to him in a monotone voice.

He looked at her, tilting his head and his eyebrows lifting a bit.

"Touché," he said, grinning, his dimples leaping out at her. "I apologize for being late, Mac."

"Thank you," Mac said, softening a bit. "We have a lot to go over, so we should get started. I thought we'd start with the outside of the store."

"Sounds strange but you're the expert. After you," he said to her, opening the door.

Mac walked through the store to the front door and stepped outside, walking until she was standing in the first parking spot in the lot.

"What do you think draws customers into the store?" she asked Blaize as he stood beside her, the two of them looking at the drab storefront.

"The name."

"You mean the logo?" she asked him.

"No, I mean the name. People come here because they know the name Van Rohrer, it's been around forever. Everyone knows us."

"Right. And the front of the store has always been like this, right? There's been no change at all. There's never been any displays or anything outside?"

"Yeah. Why?"

"You've heard of McDonalds, right? And Burger King, Kentucky Fried Chicken, places like that?" Mac asked.

"Duh. Who hasn't?"

"They have all changed with the times. McDonald's started out with just hamburgers, then added other foods on as the market dictated. They invested six billion just in the United States a few years ago to change the overall look of each location, the furniture, décor, kiosks. The same goes for your competitors. They are adapting to the market changes, and that's why they're still making so much profit after all of these years."

"So, what you're trying to say to me is that just because the store worked this way thirty years ago it doesn't mean it works now," Blaize said.

"Bingo," Mac replied.

"So, what do I do?" Blaize asked, crossing his arms. He was wearing a black polo shirt and as he crossed his arms Mac could see the bottom of a tattoo on his left bicep.

"Well, I would suggest that you dress the front up a bit for each season. For example, it's summer, so something bright out front. Not gaudy, just a little bit of oomph, if you know what I mean."

"I don't, but I'll figure it out, I guess," Blaize said. "Is that it?"

"What? No, that is far from it, Blaize. There's a ton that needs to change. Let's go inside," Mac said, frustrated. Did he really think that was all she'd been hired to do? Had the Van Rohrer's not explained to him that she had about a month of work ahead of her, all of which he was heavily involved in? She hoped they had, otherwise she really had her work cut out for her.

***

"No Rigsy?"

Mac shook her head no as she tossed back the shot, wincing after she swallowed it.

"He's at the State Police Academy," she said to Bryan, the bartender at Russo's. "He'll be home in around three weeks."

"She's counting down the days," Mads joked. "One more round of those shots, please."

"No," Mac said, waving her hands. "Not for me. I don't want to be hungover tomorrow."

They'd had two Kamikaze shots and the vodka, triple sec and lime juice had her head spinning already. After spending hours with Blaize earlier she'd wanted nothing more than to unwind at Russo's with some greasy food and strong drinks.

"Party pooper!" Mads scolded, tossing back another shot.

"Thank God," Mac said as Bryan slid her dinner over to her. She hadn't eaten all day and drinking shots on an empty stomach wasn't the best idea. She eagerly took a bite out of her cheeseburger then dipped a waffle fry in ketchup.

"Have you been checking your phone nonstop too?" Mads asked her.

"For what?" Mac asked.

"To see if the you know what hit the fan, if Tracy told about what happened."

"Who would she even tell?" Mac asked. "If you think about it, it's stupid. What's she going to do, call the police and tell them? It was over four years ago. Besides, there's no proof unless we all admit to it. I don't think she knows about it at all, I think she was just trying to cause drama like you said."

"I hope so," Mads shrugged. "Emma's worried about it and I feel like it's hanging over all of our heads."

"Well, that's because it is," Mac said, annoyed. "I told Rigsy, and he was pretty mad about it, but what can we do? Nothing, that's what." There wasn't anything they could do if Tracy did know about it, aside from wait to see if she told the police.

"Hello, ladies."

Mac looked in the mirror across from her at the bar as Rylan hugged Mads from behind, Mads taking one of her French fries and feeding it to him. She was glad for the interruption, she didn't want to talk about the what ifs of Tracy telling the secret.

"Oh great. I'm the third wheel. Again," Mac said sarcastically, grinning at Rylan.

"No way. You're my favorite, you're not a third wheel," Rylan told her, hugging her. She couldn't help but notice that he smelled really good, and it made her miss Rigsy more than she already did. Not being able to talk to him every day made her miserable, especially now that she was working. She needed to talk to someone about the challenges she was facing and not knowing when she'd hear from Rigsy left her keeping it all bottled inside.

"Thanks," Mac said as Mads moved over so Rylan could sit between the two of them.

"Any word from Rigsy?" Rylan asked Mac as Bryan slid a large glass filled with beer in front of Rylan.

"Not really. We've talked once, he isn't supposed to use his phone while he's going through the academy," Mac sighed.

"Aww, tough break. Don't worry, he'll be back before you know it," Rylan said.

"Hi."

Mac spun around on the barstool as she saw Emma and Mark, throwing her arms in the air dramatically.

"You're in public!" she exclaimed.

"Uhm, yes. Don't make us regret it please," Emma whispered loudly to Mac.

"Drink up!" Mads handed a shot to Emma and Mark as Bryan slid one in front of Mac and Rylan.

"To the fifth wheel!" Mac shouted, poking fun of herself, and drinking back the shot.

The bar was busy, the after-dinner crowd arriving, eager for strong drinks and music. Mac chatted with the locals, laughing alongside them as vacationers tried their best shot at singing karaoke. The drinks kept flowing, thanks to Rylan and Mark, who paid for all of Mac's drinks, and Mac eventually found herself up on stage with Emma and Mads, singing "Livin' on a Prayer" by Bon Jovi.

"TAKE MY HAND, WE'LL MAKE IT I SWEAR!" she screamed into the microphone, laughing as she clung onto Emma and Mads.

Rylan extended his hand to help her off of the stage when the trio was done, and Mac stumbled, winding up in his arms as he caught her.

"Whoopsie! I'm tired," she said, her head spinning. She'd lost count of how many shots she had, but knew it was too many.

"Okay, let's get you upstairs," Rylan said to her, looking around for Mads.

"Are you okay?" Mads asked Mac.

"Sure!" Mac replied enthusiastically.

"I think she needs to go to bed," Rylan said to Mads, grinning as he held Mac up.

"Definitely. Let's go," Mads said, moving alongside Mac and helping to walk her out of the bar. "Em, save my seat!"

Mac giggled and waved goodbye to Bryan and the others as Mads and Rylan carried her out of the bar and around the corner to the stairway to the apartment.

"You two, you two would have such beautiful babies," Mac slurred as they carried her carefully up the stairs.

"Oh my God Mac," Mads laughed. "Stop."

"Really! They would have such pretty eyes!" Mac insisted.

"Okay, put her on the couch while I get her some water," Mads told Rylan.

"Weeeeee!" Mac sang as Rylan sat her on the chaise part of the sectional.

"Drink this," Mads instructed Mac as she handed her a bottle of Gatorade. "You need the electrolytes."

Mac drank some of the punch flavored drink, frowning as she swallowed it.

"Yuck," she said, holding out the bottle and looking at it.

"Here," Mads handed her a bag of potato chips. "Do you want us to stay with you?"

"Pffft," Mac said, shooing them away with her hands. "I'm not a baby! Go have fun, I'm gonna take a nap."

"If you need us we'll be right downstairs," Rylan told her.

"Okay dad."

"I'll come check on you in a bit," Mads told Mac, laughing as Mac saluted them before they left.

Mac laid on the chaise, listening to the sounds of the bar drift up through the open slider. She gulped down some more of the Gatorade and sat up straight, reaching for her phone to call Rigsy.

"Ugh," she said out loud. Rigsy couldn't get calls, he wouldn't be able to talk.

She wanted to tell him about her first day at the Van Rohrer's, about Blaize with a z. The music switched from a rowdy version of Love Shack to a sappy love song, and she stared at her phone, scrolling through her contacts. Stopping on one she clicked on the name and then sent a text, placing the phone down on her lap after she did and closing her eyes.

CHAPTER NINE

The smell of food cooking on the grill made Mac's stomach growl as she and Mads walked to the back of Mac's parent's house. Her head was throbbing from the night before and she hoped some food would help get rid of the massive hangover that she had.

"Mr. Walsh those steaks smell awesome," Mads said as she sat down on the picnic table.

"There's steak, chicken breast, and peppers and onions. I expect you girls to take some home with you to Emma, she's stuck working at the store," Mac's father said as he flipped the steaks, the flame from the grill jumping up as he did. "Of course, that's assuming Rylan here doesn't eat everything."

"I'll try not to," Rylan joked, shaking Mac's father's hand. "Thanks for having me over again."

"We love having you over Rylan, you're welcome any time, and I'm not just saying that because you're one of the store's top customers," Mac's father said. "Grab yourself a beer from that cooler over there if you want."

"Ugh," Mac said, turning green at the thought of alcohol.

"Hi everyone," Mac's mom said as she appeared from the house carrying a large tray with more food. "I've got some macaroni salad and potato salad here, I made extra so you can take some home. Poor Emma is still working."

"Mom, we get it. We will bring all of the leftovers home so Emma can stuff her face when she gets out of work," Mac laughed, reaching for the macaroni salad.

"I just feel bad that she's working so much. I've told her she can hire on more help, but she doesn't want to," Mac's mom said as she sat down.

"She loves working there, don't worry about it, Mrs. Walsh," Mads said, scooching over on the picnic table so Rylan could sit next to her.

"Well, you know who has been in a lot more than usual lately and I worry she'll want to quit because of it," Mac's mom said in a loud whisper.

Mac and Mads looked at each other.

"You know who?" Mac asked her mom, laughing.

"Yes," her mother replied, focusing on the potato salad that she was plopping onto Mac's plate.

"Mom. We don't know who you know who is, can you possibly tell us?" Mac asked.

"It's Mark. Who else would it be?" Mac's mom asked, frowning.

"Uh, I don't know, anyone? Besides, I don't think Mark going to the store bugs Emma. Don't worry about it."

"Yeah Mrs. Walsh, Emma's fine. I'm pretty sure that she can handle Mark," Mads said, looking at Mac. The two girls laughed as Mac's parents shrugged.

"Any word from Rigsy?" her dad asked as he put the food from the grill onto a platter.

"He can't talk much while he's there, they don't like them to use their phones. I've texted a few times with him, and we talked once. He loves it so far," Mac said, taking a chicken breast off of the platter. "His only complaint is that it's so hot, there's no air conditioning where they are sleeping."

"It's so exciting, him becoming a State Trooper," Mac's mom said, sounding like a giddy school girl.

"Well, he isn't one yet, don't jinx it," Mac said.

"I'm excited because now I can get out of tickets by dropping his name," Mads said matter of factly, the smile on her face fading as she looked at Mac's parent's serious faces. "Uh, I am joking, of course. I don't get tickets."

"Madison, I remember when you were about thirteen, you wouldn't stop riding your bicycle in the middle of the street instead of on the side. You'd ride that bike smack down the middle of Main Street. Everyone was in an uproar over it, not just for safety reasons but the traffic jam it always caused. And finally, Jim Edmonds, who was a police officer at the time, pulled you over and wrote you a ticket," Mac's mom had a grin on her face as she told the story.

"Ha! Did she really?" Rylan asked, elbowing Mads.

"Oh my God! I remember that, too! You used to pop a wheelie on your bike and ride it down the road," Mac said, laughing at the memory. "Sometimes you'd do it with no hands, too."

"I still don't think giving a kid a ticket for riding a bike is legal!" Mads argued, laughing. "Also, I was good on that bike. I did all kinds of stunts, so it was like giving people a free show."

"Except you were in the middle of traffic, and most of them had to swerve to avoid hitting you, or they'd slow down to five miles an hour afraid to pass you. I know because I got stuck behind them more than once!" Mac's father said, laughing.

Mac smiled as she watched her parents laugh, happy that they were enjoying themselves. A few months ago, she wouldn't have been so sure that they would be enjoying life again, but the store was doing better than she'd ever have expected it to, all of the past rent was paid in full and there was now a healthy amount in savings for them. They loved being at the store, chatting with the locals and helping the people that were staying from out of town with recommendations on where to eat and the best time to snag a parking space at the beach.

"We have some exciting news," Mac's mom said.

Mac looked at her mom, unsure of what the news could possibly be. They were too old to have another kid, that was for sure.

"We're semi-retiring!" Mac's father announced, a huge smile on his face.

"Congratulations!" Rylan said as he dug into the chicken.

"Wow! That's great!" Mads said excitedly as she cut into her steak.

"Thank you, Madison. Your parents have encouraged it for a while," Mac's mom said. "They've tried to get us to go down to their place for years!"

"Uh, this is great and all but what exactly do you mean by semi-retired? You guys are at the store all day, every day. What are you going to do? And who's going to run the store when you're gone?" Mac asked, starting to get a pit in her stomach.

"Well, we realized that life is short, and we sure aren't getting any younger. Your father's hip has healed but it bothers him when a lot when it's raining and imagine what it will be like with the snow and frigid winter weather when it rolls in. So, we talked about maybe going down south for the winter."

Mac looked at her mother and then her father, dumbfounded. They had never talked about this, ever. At least not to her.

"Maybe you can stay with my parents, their house is big enough. They have a whole separate part with its own entrance and kitchen, so it'd be like an apartment. I bet they'd love to have you!" Mads said excitedly.

"Actually, that's the plan. Your parents have generously offered for us to stay with them. We'll come back for the holidays, of course or maybe Mac will fly down to see us," Mac's mom said, looking at Mac. "It's only a three-hour flight."

"Hold on," Mac said, holding her hands up. "Before you start planning this, who is going to run the store and look after things if you're gone for the winter?"

Her parents looked at each other before her dad spoke up.

"Well, we were hoping that you would."

****

Mac sat on the deck, throwing Cheerios to Sammy. Her head was spinning over the bomb her parents had dropped on her about semi-retiring and spending a few months in Florida, and she'd called Rigsy to talk about it, but as usual he had yet to call her back.

Getting the job for the Van Rohrer's was huge for her, but it was only for a month. She was hoping that it would lead to other similar stores wanting to hire her, but if she had to manage Walsh's Market on Main then she could only commit to working for two months for a client until she'd have to work at the store through March. Having a five month gap didn't exactly scream that she was running a professional business.

Her phone rang and she answered it at once, eager to talk to Rigsy about her parents semi-retiring. She could use some advice and a shoulder to cry on.

"Hi, I'm so happy you called," she said excitedly.

"Me too."

Mac froze for a minute and then held the phone out so that she could see who the caller was.

Austin.

Her heart started to race, and she vaguely remembered texting him the night before. Oh God. She'd forgotten all about doing it.

"Mackenzie?" Austin asked.

"Yes, sorry. Uh, it's good to hear from you."

"Is now a good time to talk? You sound pre-occupied."

"Oh, no. It's fine, I can talk," Mac said, stumbling through her words.

"I was surprised to hear from you. I take it you got my letter?"

"Yes, I did," Mac said. She wasn't sure what to say to him and was starting to think maybe it hadn't been a good idea to unblock him. This was awkward.

"Mackenzie, I.."

"You don't have to explain anything," she interrupted. "The letter explained it all. I…I guess I just felt like we didn't get any closure with how I left. At least I didn't."

"I agree. I tried to call you and email you, you know. You blocked me."

"I know. I guess I just wanted to move on at the time," Mac said.

"And now you don't?" Austin asked.

"No, I do. I have, I mean," Mac said. She didn't want Austin to get the impression that she was giving him another chance. "Austin, I'm in a relationship with someone."

She felt relieved by telling him, as if it somehow made it okay for her to have texted him. Did it? She wasn't so sure, but by telling him that she was in a relationship he would know that she wasn't interested in a relationship with him. At least she hoped he would.

"Oh. Well, I guess I'm confused. I called you because you texted me, I thought you wanted to talk. And you just said you didn't get any closure with us," Austin said, sounding slightly irritated.

Mac closed her eyes and vowed to never drink shots again, they led to nothing but trouble.

"Austin, the truth is that I just don't understand how you thought I would be okay with not working and being a stay-at-home wife. We had so many talks about our future, and not once did I mention leaving my career. Or, not even starting it. I guess it just made me question if all of that was just talk from you, that you weren't even listening to me and just went along with what I said because you planned on changing it anyway. Did you think that I couldn't do it? Get a real job, I mean? Do you think I can't be successful in business?" The thought had crossed Mac's mind lately that maybe she wasn't cut out to be a businesswoman. Sure, she'd worked in California, but that was at a café and as an intern. The internship wasn't easy, she was a hard worker there, but it wasn't a real job. And since then she hadn't exactly lit the world on fire with her work ethic.

"Mackenzie, I listened to my parents too much is what I did. Of course I think you could get a real job. I did plan on us having careers, each of us, but you know how my parents are. I made a huge mistake that night. Overall, I was selfish, and I know that now. But if you're with someone else I guess none of this matters much, does it?"

"Well, it matters to me. We were together for four years, don't you think we should be friends?"

"Friends?"

"I know it sounds lame, Austin. I guess I just thought that since we were with each other for so long it would be nice to be on good terms. I don't hate you, and that's how I left you in my opinion, with hate. So, I just wanted you to know I will always think about our time together fondly, and I don't have any bad feelings towards you."

"This means a lot to me. Obviously, the fact you're in a relationship isn't what I wanted to hear, but it is what it is. I'd like for us to be friends, too, Mackenzie."

"Well, now that we've got that covered, how have you been?" Mac blurted out, laughing.

"I've been good," Austin said, laughing. "I decided to take the summer off, actually, so I've just been hanging around at the beach and stuff."

"What! You, at the beach? Not working? I don't believe it! Your parents must have lost their minds!" Mac said.

"Yup," Austin said, laughing. "But they're cool with it now. I start work after Labor Day. What about you?"

"Well, I started my own business. Right now, I'm working on updating one of the Van Rohrer's stores, the original one actually."

"Really? What do you mean, updating?"

"Almost like a re-branding of sorts." Mac explained in detail about what she had planned for the Van Rohrer's, and then about her parents wanting to semi-retire. She was excited to be able to talk to someone who had an interest in business about what she was doing, and Austin understood the complexity of a company's finances and was able to offer goof advice. The more she spoke the less guilty she felt about talking to him, it felt natural.

Just because they were exes it didn't mean they couldn't be friends, right?

CHAPTER TEN

"I don't think that's going to make any difference at all. What a waste of money."

Mac could feel her face getting red as she ignored Blaize and continued to toss items from the shelves into the large bin. It was ten at night and she had a long night ahead of her. Working at the Van Rohrer's when the store was closed was the most productive, although Blaize hadn't been thrilled about it and was doing nothing but complaining.

"Blaize, this stuff is so outdated. How long has it been sitting on the shelf? I mean, look at this," Mac picked up one of the perfume bottles and blew on it, causing a puff of dust to swirl up off of it. "How are you making money if this is sitting here for months? Replace it with stuff that sells. What the heck is Jean Nate, anyway?"

"Ask my mom, she's the one that bought it all."

"Thirty years ago. This is the issue, Blaize. The products that your mom bought for the store thirty years ago don't sell now. People don't want Jean Nate, they want Bath and Body Works. At some point what you ordered should have changed, when you see the same products sitting on the shelves month on end and no one's buying them it's time to look at new stuff. And, for the record, this isn't a waste of money. What I am doing will cost up front but bring in more revenue over the long run."

"Whatever you say," Blaize said, picking up a bottle of Ralph Lauren cologne. "So, I should just toss this, right?"

"No. That's a classic, people still buy it. You run the store, why don't you know what people buy from here?"

"I do, I just wasn't sure if this is popular enough for you."

"Blaize, you're wearing a Ralph Lauren shirt, Rag and Bone jeans, and Gucci loafers. You obviously know a bit about fashion. Drop the sarcasm, stop acting clueless, and step it up. I'm doing my job and even though you're the owner's son I get the feeling that if you don't do your job, too, you might be without one soon."

She walked away, leaving him standing with his mouth open. She'd had enough of him. He challenged every change that she wanted to make, arguing with her about it until her ears felt like they would bleed. It was like working with a toddler and she wasn't sure how much longer she could put up with him.

She stepped outside for a break and walked to her car where she'd left a mini cooler with some water and iced coffee. She needed the caffeine to stay up. She'd spent the last few nights talking to Austin on the phone after leaving the Van Rohrer's store and hadn't gotten enough sleep.

She sipped some of the cold brew as she looked around the empty parking lot. Her nerves were on edge, she was worried about her parents plan to semi-retire and how she needed to help them, and she was also feeling a bit guilty about talking to Austin. At the same time, their talks had been completely innocent, focusing on work and life in general. She hadn't heard from Rigsy, and she didn't see the harm in talking to Austin as long as it didn't cross the line into flirting, which it hadn't.

Her phone hummed with an incoming text, and she looked at the screen and laughed. Austin had sent a funny meme to her.

"Are we done?"

Mac looked at Blaize, who was standing in the store's doorway.

"NO!" she yelled back, rolling her eyes as she took the cooler out of the car and walked back towards the store. It was going to be a long night.

****

"What's the ruckus?" Mac asked as she walked into the living room. She'd just woken up after working at the Van Rohrer's store until four that morning. They'd accomplished a lot, getting rid of all of what Mac called dead inventory.

"Rylan's leaving," Emma said. She was sitting on the couch, surrounded with material to make her bags. Mads was next to her, a box of Kleenex on her lap.

"Leaving?" Mac asked as she shuffled over to the kitchen for some coffee.

"He's got his next job after he's done at the resort, a bunch of houses down in York," Mads said. Her eyes were swollen and bloodshot, she'd clearly been crying. Mac couldn't remember the last time that she'd seen Mads cry, never mind over a guy.

"Oh no," Mac said, trying not to sound uninterested. Mads had to have known that this would happen, it wasn't as if Rylan's job at the resort was permanent. He'd been hired through the summer, after that his work there was done.

"Go ahead, say it," Mads told her, sniffling. "Tell me I told you so. You said I should tell him how I felt, and now it's too late. He's leaving."

"You can still tell him, Mads," Mac said, opening up the cabinets as she looked for the sugar.

"Why bother now!" Mads said angrily.

Mac and Emma exchanged glances. Mads hadn't ever acted like this over a guy before, she was always easy breezy and casual, never looking at the future and just living day to day.

"Mads, if you tell him maybe that will change his mind about leaving. That's why you should bother," Mac said as she settled on Splenda instead of sugar for her coffee.

"If he liked me he would have said something," Mads said, picking at the ends of her hair.

"He has! All summer! Every time you two have been together he's hinted around about a future, and you blow him off," Emma reminded Mads. "It's almost mean, to be honest."

"That's not true," Mads snapped, standing up to walk to the kitchen.

"Uh, yes actually, it is," Mac said, grabbing her coffee along with a days old Danish and sitting down. "Just last week he talked about the two of you going to the Holiday Stroll, and you laughed and reminded him he'd be long gone, and you'd already have replaced him by then."

"I was joking!" Mads exclaimed, taking a gallon of mint chocolate chip ice cream out of the freezer.

"Well, I think when you always joke like that the person eventually assumes that it actually isn't a joke," Emma said, picking up a piece of teal material and cutting it. "I don't understand why you still haven't told him you have feelings for him."

"He isn't a mind reader, Mads. You should tell him how you feel, and not in a jokey, ha ha, way. Say it in an adult way, like maybe go out for a nice dinner or a drive down the coast," Mac suggested.

Mads plopped back down on the couch, digging into the ice cream container with a spoon.

"I need more space," Emma sighed as she stood up and looked around. "I have way too much material and need to space it all out so I can make these bags faster."

"You can use my room if you want. Lay it out on my bed and use my desk to put them together, maybe?" Mac offered to Emma.

"Yeah, I'll use your room if that's okay. Thanks," Emma said as she started to pick all of the materials up. "How's it going with the Van Rohrer's, anyway? You weren't home when I got here and that was around two this morning."

"It's been bumpy. Blaize, the GM who is also their son, is fighting me on everything I do. But we're making progress," Mac said as her phone went off. She glanced down at the screen and discretely pulled a throw pillow over the phone. Austin was calling her, and she didn't want Emma or Mads to know that she'd been talking to him, they'd get the wrong idea.

"Uh, excuse me who was that?" Mads asked, sitting up straight and craning her neck towards the throw pillow.

"No one," Mac said nonchalantly, hoping Mads would drop it.

"You sure about that?" Mads asked as Mac's phone went off again. Mac flipped the throw pillow over and her jaw dropped.

"MACKENZIE WALSH!" she yelled, her eyes wide open. "You little sneak!"

"What's going on?" Emma asked, her arms full of material.

"She's been talking to Austin," Mads said.

"Seriously?" Emma asked, looking at Mac. "And you gave me a hard time about Mark?"

"Whoa, hold on. I'm not dating Austin again. I'm not sneaking him in at night. He sent me a letter, and I may or may not have texted him after having a few too many shots the night we were at Russo's singing Bon Jovi."

"Yikes," Mads said. "I'm going to go out on a limb and assume Rigsy doesn't know?"

"Absolutely not, and no one should mention it to him, either. Not that we are doing anything inappropriate, because we aren't."

Mac caught Emma and Mads looking at each other and knew what they were thinking. She would think the same thing if she were in their shoes, too.

"Look, I made a mistake. I haven't been able to talk to Rigsy much since he left, and I was lonely. It was stupid of me," Mac explained.

"We didn't say anything," Emma said, her voice trailing off as she went into Mac's room.

"You didn't have to, I can read it on your faces," Mac said loudly, looking at Mads.

"I'm not one to give relationship advice, for obvious reasons, but Rigsy is a pretty cool guy and you two seem to have a lot going for you. You might want to nip this in the bud with Austin, because no matter how innocent it is, if Rigsy finds out it won't go over well."

Mac started to say something and then stopped, digesting what Mads had said.

For someone who had never been in a relationship before, she had just given some spot-on advice.

CHAPTER ELEVEN

"I know it hasn't been that long, but I wanted to see what you thought so far. You know, just to make sure that I'm on the right track."

Mac forced a smile as she leaned up against her car.

"Well, you seem really thrilled to be here," Blaize said to her as the two stood in the parking lot at Van Rhorer's, facing the store.

"Sorry," Mac mumbled. Her outfit matched her mood, she was dressed in all black, and her hair was in a messy bun because she hadn't had the energy to style it. She'd spent two hours on the phone with Austin the night before and hadn't slept afterwards because she had felt guilty about it. She needed to stop talking to him, he'd started to cross the line with flirting, and that wasn't anything that she wanted to entertain. Mads had been right, so much for just being friends, it clearly wasn't that easy.

"Well, what do you think?" he asked, extending his arms out towards the store front.

The dull storefront had been brought to life with teal, peach, and red Adirondack chairs lining the walkway in front of it. Vibrant potted plants sat in between each chair, creating a far more welcoming display than the empty space had before. The windows had dozens of colorful flowery wreaths hung on them, all in varying sizes.

"The plants and wreaths are the faux ones you suggested we sell, they came in early this morning," Blaize said.

"It looks great," Mac said, forcing another smile. She wanted to be at home, so she could eat a gallon of ice cream while staring at her phone, waiting for Rigsy to call, and hoping that Austin didn't.

"Thanks," Blaize replied, sounding a bit defeated.

Mac immediately felt bad. Blaize had done exactly what she'd advised, even though he hadn't wanted to, and instead of being positive about it she was mopey.

"I'm sorry if I seem negative, it isn't anything to do with the store. This looks great, really. I'm excited to see what you did inside."

His face lit up, and she walked with him into the store, taking a deep breath while reminding herself this was her job. She needed to leave her personal issues at the door.

Although there was more work for them to do, while Mac had been busy working with the purchasing department Blaize had taken the initiative and cleaned up and started organizing the interior of the store. There were no more clothes or shoes scattered on the floor, and the clothes on the racks had been thinned out so that they weren't jammed in next to each other.

The shoe section had been set up similar to one of the photos she had shown him, with displays lining up the front and tops of each row, with benches to sit down on running down the middle.

"This looks really good," Mac said as she walked down one of the shoe aisles. "I like that you can see over the racks, that they aren't super tall I mean. Did you have these racks in storage or something?"

"In storage," Blaize replied. "I thought it would open the area up more, too."

"It definitely did."

"You know, I have a friend who makes beach bags, they sell them at the Sandy Shore and a few other local stores," Mac said, eyeing the display of handbags that was on the wall. "I think they'd do well here. They're nice, not gaudy, and they're made locally. I mentioned having some locally made items here, that'd be a step. If you're interested, of course."

"Sure, that'd be great, actually. I just wish I had thought of the new layout and inventory stuff instead of someone having to be hired to suggest it. No offense, of course."

"No offense taken," Mac said, smiling. "I think the Van Rohrer's just wanted to see results fast, that's all."

"It's okay to tell me if they said I was a disappointment, it wouldn't be the first time. They're my parents."

Mac put down the Nike sneakers she had in her hands and turned to look at him. "Hold on. Mandy and Bob Van Rohrer are your parents?"

"Yep."

"I didn't know that," Mac said, feeling foolish after she did. It wasn't as if she would treat him any differently if she'd known that he was their son. She just found it odd that they never mentioned it, even when talking about him they had used his title versus calling him their son. All of her research hadn't revealed that they had a son working for them, either, although she hadn't specifically looked for that and had focused more on the sales aspect of the business.

"Most people don't" he said, shrugging. "It isn't like we announce it."

"Do you not want to work for them or something?" Mac asked. "It seems like you don't have much interest in running the store."

"Well, I did go to school for business," Blaize said defensively.

"Oh. So, that's a yes then? You do want to work for them?"

"That's a yes until I met my girlfriend at college. I wanted to stay there after graduation, but that wasn't part of my parent's plan."

"Where'd you go to school?"

"University of California, San Diego."

"Oh boy," Mac said, laughing. "Small world. I went to UC Los Angeles. I graduated a few months ago."

"Get out. Really?" Blaize asked, grinning.

"Yes. And, I also had plans to stay in California after graduation. My boyfriend lived there. Uh, I mean ex-boyfriend."

"Hmm. Ex-boyfriend. What happened?"

"My dad broke his hip, so I came back here to help out for a week and ended up realizing I wanted to stay here. It's kind of a long story, I ended up getting back together with my boyfriend from high school. What happened with you?"

"I agreed to come home for the summer after graduation, and my girlfriend, Alexandria, came with me. Things were great, but after it snowed for the first time she said she couldn't live here and left."

"Hmm. I can't say that I blame her," Mac said. "Sorry, bad joke. So, is that why you haven't really done much with the store?"

"I guess," he shrugged. "It happened last year, and I guess I just felt like it was my parent's fault. Her leaving me, I mean. "

"Your parents didn't make it snow," Mac said.

"Obviously. I'm talking about if they had just let me stay in California then we probably wouldn't have broken up. They insisted that I come back here to be the General Manager. I worked here until I left for college, but not as a manager."

"And what would you be doing for work if you had stayed in California?" Mac asked, curious to know if he had a job lined up after graduation. She got the feeling he didn't.

Blaize stood in silence, pursing his lips a bit, and shifting his weight from one leg to the other.

"I'd have found a job, I know that," he said.

"Right, but would it be as the General Manager for a well-known store chain?" Mac asked. "I don't think any company would just give someone with minimal experience, if any, such a high-level job."

"Probably not."

"Blaize, you realize you have a great opportunity, right? To turn this place around. And if you are successful, then you could possibly open another store out on the west coast, right? Not that you want to live there anymore, but you see my point."

"The thought has crossed my mind, to expand our presence. I guess I've just focused too much on blaming my parents for making me come back."

"I hate to be so blunt, but your girlfriend leaving you because she couldn't stand the snow for a few months out of the year doesn't really scream solid relationship to me. You're better off without her. Trust me," Mac said.

"You're probably right. Then again it's easy for you to say because you're back with your high school sweetheart," Blaize teased. "It's nice that you came back for him."

"No, I didn't come back for him, I really came back because my dad broke his hip. On my first day back, I was pulled over by the police, and it turned out to be him. Totally random. I know it sounds corny."

"He's a cop?"

"Yup. In Summer Cove. Well, he was, now he's at the State Police Academy."

"Wow, that's great. My Uncle Steve is a statie! Good pension, he talks about retiring in a year all the time. Where will your boyfriend be stationed?"

"Huh?" Mac asked, unsure of what Blaize meant.

"Where will he work from the first year? I think they get assigned to an area in the state, right? My Uncle is in Washington County, up where Forest is. He lived here but ended up moving to Forest because he liked it so much."

Mac stood in silence, trying to digest what Blaize had just told her. Rigsy hadn't mentioned this at all, that he would be stationed anywhere in the state of Maine. She had assumed he would be working near Summer Cove.

Forest, Maine was almost five hours from Summer Cove, and there were other towns in Maine that were even farther away than that.

What if he wound up there?

****

The sound of people singing karaoke at Russo's floated into the apartment, the noise resembling a screeching parrot.

"That is absolutely horrible," Mads groaned. "Wanna go down and make fun of them?"

"No," Mac answered as she cross checked the inventory lists on her laptop.

"You've been grouchy since you got home. What's going on?" Mads asked, sitting on the living room floor in front of the sectional.

"I'm not grouchy, I'm just annoyed."

"Uh, okay. Whatever you are, do you want to tell me or is this something you'll get over by tomorrow, because having you mope around here gives me anxiety."

"It's Rigsy," Mac said, closing her laptop and pulling her legs up onto the couch.

"What about him?"

"Apparently, he can be stationed anywhere in the entire state for the first year of his job as a State Trooper."

"Clarify apparently, either he can or cannot, which is it? How does he not know?" Mads asked.

"He didn't tell me, Blaize did."

"Blaize? Who the heck is Blaize?" Mads asked, laughing.

"The Van Rohrer's son, I told you about him. He's the General Manager for their stores. His uncle is on the force."

"Is that his real name, Blaize? Or is that short for something else? Is his real name Blazer?" Mads asked, giggling.

"Can you focus on what I'm telling you and stop asking about Blaize?"

"You're right, sorry. Okay, so Rigsy might live somewhere else in the state for the first year. That's not horrible, is it?"

"Uh, it is if he gets sent near the border. He could be five or six hours away."

"Yikes. I always forget that Maine is so big. What does that mean for you guys? Would you go live with him?"

"No. I think he lives at a house with other troopers or something, I'm not sure."

"So, you'd just see each other on holidays or something?"

"I think he'll be working on the holidays, he has since he's been on the force."

"Good grief," Mads said. "I feel like you two aren't on the same page. No wonder you've been talking to Austin."

"Oh my God! Mads!" Emma scolded.

"You know, it kind of stinks not having my boyfriend around and being stuck with you two. Emma, you have Mark, and your bag business and the store and Mads you have the resort and Rylan. I feel like I'm flailing around over here alone."

"How can you say that? You're literally working for one of the most well-known stores on the east coast," Mads said.

"Yeah Mac, I know it stinks that Rigsy is away, but it isn't like you don't have anything going on, you're doing good so far with business," Emma said.

"Am I? Because basically after I finish the Van Rohrer's I have two months until my parents will need me at the store every day. So, what do I do then? Tell clients I'll see them in the spring? And what if Rigsy gets stationed way up north? I just see him a few times a year or something?"

Mac stood up, frustrated. She hated that she had no answers to her questions.

Hi beautiful

She sighed heavily as she read the text from Austin. She also hated that she had unblocked him, and while she had no answers for her other problems she did have one for this.

CHAPTER TWELVE

"I won't lie, when you said beach bags I was picturing those big, ugly straw ones," Blaize said as he held up one of the bags that Emma made.

Mac grinned as she stood in the lobby store at the Sandy Shore. She'd met Blaize for a working breakfast and then they'd gone there so he could see a few of Emma's bags.

"They're unique, aren't they? Emma, my friend who makes them, has started to call them all purpose totes instead of beach bags. You can use them for anything, really. Beach bags, work, whatever. My favorite ones are the ones with sea glass or metals sewn into them."

"The ones with the metal have a cool urban feel," Blaize said. "I'm going to buy this one to show my mother, and then place an order with your friend."

"Is that the last one?"

Mac ignored Tracy, who was standing behind Blaize, hoping that she'd go away. Instead, she stepped closer to them, reaching for the last bag on the display.

"Oh, sorry," Blaize said, stepping aside." You have good taste."

"Me?" Tracy asked, batting her thick black eyelashes, and tossing her hair over her shoulder.

Mac tried not to roll her eyes as she introduced them to each other.

"Blaize, that's a unique name," Tracy said." Is that with an S or a Z?"

"It's with a Z. Nice seeing you, Tracy" Mac said, hoping to get rid of her.

"How do you two know each other?" Blaize asked.

Mac and Tracy looked at each other, neither one saying anything until Mac finally broke the silence. "We went to school together."

"You went to UCLA too?" Blaize asked Tracy. "I went to UC San Diego!"

"Uh, no. High School. Well, technically all schools, right Mac? We both grew up here in town," Tracy told Blaize.

"Tracy owns the nail salon next door," Mac said.

"That's great!" Blaize said excitedly.

Mac looked at him, suddenly realizing what was going on. He was way too excited over a nail salon. He was hitting on Tracy. And Tracy loved it. She had to, since when would she buy something that Emma had made?

"Thanks. You should come sometime, men can get manicures too, you know," Tracy said to him, winking.

"I just might do that," Blaize said, flashing his smile at her.

His phone went off and he frowned as he looked at it.

"I have to get back to the store. Mac, I'll call you later. It was great meeting you, Tracy."

Mac shot Tracy a dirty look as Tracy watched Blaize walk out of the store into the resort lobby to leave. For a split second she considered asking Tracy what the secret was that she knew, challenging her and calling her bluff, but then decided against it.

"Who is he?"

Mac stopped walking, turning to look at Tracy, who had followed her out of the store into the lobby.

"A client," Mac said dryly, stepping aside as a large group of people entered the lobby. They were all sunburned and looked like they had drunk a bit too much of whatever was inside the coolers they were lugging behind them.

"Well, he isn't from around here. I'd remember him if he was," Tracy said.

"Tracy, do you need something? Aside from trying to find out who Blaize is, I mean. A few days ago, you basically threatened me here, now you're acting like nothing happened."

"Ahem."

Mac looked over at the front desk, where Mads was working. She nodded her head towards Tracy's salon as she checked in a family of six, who were arguing about not getting a discount for being repeat customers.

"We can't talk in the lobby," Mac said, turning to leave.

"Let's go in my salon," Tracy suggested, pulling the door open.

Mac hesitated. On one hand, she had no interest in talking to Tracy. On the other, she was curious to see if Tracy wanted to ask more questions about Blaize or talk about something else, like the secret that she allegedly knew.

Opting for the latter, she stepped inside Tracy's salon and looked around.

The space was long and narrow, but Tracy had set it up to her advantage. There were four manicure stations and two pedicure chairs on the left-hand side, and the mirrored wall across from them had floating shelves that held dozens of colors of nail polish. There were accents around the space, two small deep purple club chairs next to the front door, a large Ficus next to the small black desk that had a cash register on it. Aside from the one wall that was mirrored the rest had white shiplap, which looked nice and brightened the space up.

"Rylan did a good job with that shiplap," Mac said, taking a seat in one of the purple chairs.

"Yes, he did."

"So, what did you want to talk about? Blaize?" Mac asked.

"No," Tracy said, sitting down next to her. "I wanted to talk about what I said the other day."

"Look Tracy, I don't want to argue with you, especially about Emma and Mark. What's done is done, and it has nothing to do with me."

"I know, Mac. I was wrong about what I said the other day."

"You were?" Mac asked, stunned with what Tracy had said. She'd expected her to be nasty and accusatory, not apologetic.

"I was mad," she said, shrugging as she leaned back in the chair. "What happened between me and Mark has nothing to do with any of you, I lashed out at the wrong people."

"Should you be lashing out at anyone at all?" Mac asked. "Tracy, Mark was still married to Emma when you hooked up with him. Now you're mad because, according to you, she hooked up with him while you two were still engaged. Explain the difference to me, why it's okay if you do it but no one else can?"

"I'm in therapy," Tracy blurted out.

Mac made a face, unsure of why Tracy would tell her that she was in therapy, it wasn't her business and it had nothing to do with their conversation.

"Uh, that's good, but I don't need to know that," Mac said.

"That didn't come out right," Tracy said, taking a deep breath. "I've been in therapy for a few months. My therapist has helped me out a lot, she's made me understand why I do and say things that sabotage others and myself. It stems from issues with my dad when he left us. I seek attention from men, it doesn't matter if they're married, or single, or even if they're gay for crying out loud. I'm working through it."

"I thought you had a good relationship with your dad?" Mac asked, unsure if she believed what Tracy was telling her. From what she remembered growing up Tracy had the perfect family.

"I do. My dad left my mom and me when I was six. He took off with his secretary. He came back a year later. You never heard this story?" Tracy asked. "I kind of figured everyone in town knew."

"No, never," Mac answered. "Honestly, I don't know how, you know how gossip flies through this town."

"My mom told everyone he was sick, that he was away getting treatment. It was horrible. All she did was cry, and sometimes he would call to talk to me and that made her worse. Every time I heard a car come down the street I ran to the window, praying it was my dad."

"That's rough for a six-year-old. I'm sorry."

"He showed up one day, coming back home like he had never left. It took me years before I stopped having anxiety attacks whenever he left the house, because no matter what he said I worried that he wouldn't come home again. Anyway, I'm not using this as an excuse. It isn't. I'm just telling you that I'm not going to tell anyone about the guard stand, and I have no issue with Emma or Mark. Holding onto this stuff isn't good for me. Besides, this town is way too small to hold a grudge."

"I agree," Mac said. "Plus, if I want my nails done I'd rather get them done here in town instead of driving half an hour away!"

The two women laughed, and Mac's heart lifted a bit. She could cross off worrying about Tracy telling people about the guard stand. She had one less thing to worry about.

CHAPTER THIRTEEN

"We don't have to do it."

Mac sighed loudly, turning to look at her mother.

"Mom, I'm not saying you shouldn't do it. I'm saying I can't commit to living here at the house while you're away. And I can't have Muckie stay at the apartment."

"Muckie just needs fresh water and food every day, he can come in and out of his dog door. You'd just need to swing by and check on him a few days a week, maybe spend some time with him," her father said.

"That's not fair to Muckie. And what about when it snows? Who's plowing your driveway? And what about Rose and the rest of the chickens?" Mac felt like the roles were reversed, and she was the parent, and her parents were the child. "It's not realistic to think that I can just swing by once or twice a week. And we haven't even touched on the fact that I might not be able to help with the store."

"I guess it's more complicated than we thought it'd be," her father said, sighing heavily. "Eh, some other time. Maybe we plan it for next year."

Mac watched as her dad got up slowly from the rocking chair, holding himself steady by grasping onto the pole on the front porch of the house. It had become obvious to her that his hip still bothered him, she'd noticed that at the store he could often be found perched on a tall stool with one leg on the floor, that way he could stand up without struggling. The fact that he wouldn't take any pain relievers didn't help, he didn't believe in them and refused to take anything aside from baby aspirin which wasn't strong enough to provide any relief.

"Dad's hip will get worse in the cold weather, won't it," she said. She wasn't necessarily asking, she already knew the answer.

"Most likely," her mother replied. "That's why I wanted to go down south. It's one thing for him to be here for a few frigid days, or even a few weeks. But four or five months straight, I just don't know how he will handle it. I worry he's going to be so stiff he will fall down those darn stairs again. Mornings are very rough for him, that's why he walks shortly after waking up. It helps loosen him up."

Guilt washed over Mac like a rogue wave. Her parents had never been to Florida, they'd never been anywhere, really. They'd worked hard to keep the store in Summer Cove, and they had been active in all of the towns and school's activities when Mac was growing up. They spent their money on things like sponsoring the little league team, pitching in to get new uniforms for the Girl Scouts, paying for the DJ at the Prom.

"We will figure a way out so you guys can go," she said.

"Mac, I don't want to push you into this. I didn't think it through all the way, Madison's folks don't have pets to worry about, they can just fly down to Florida without any worries. Or they could afford to pay someone to housesit if they did. Also, Madison works there at the resort, she doesn't have her own business like you do. We can go next year like your dad said. That way we have enough time to figure out coverage."

"No, you will go this year. You need to for dad's health. Besides, you guys deserve to have some time off. Something I was thinking about was if you've ever thought of asking Emma to manage the store? She already kind of does, right? Why not make it official?"

"You wouldn't be mad?"

"Mad? Mom, no, I wouldn't be mad. I don't want to be the manager at the store. No offense, it just isn't what I want to do for a career. And I think Emma deserves it, she's good at it and she likes it there."

"Your father and I just weren't sure if you would change your mind about your career. You had a lot of free time this summer, we thought maybe you'd had second thoughts about starting your business," Mac's mom said as she scratched Muckie behind the ear.

"I haven't had second thoughts. I just had a bumpy start."

"Well, if you're certain you won't be upset, I do agree that Emma deserves to have a manager title. She's a very hard worker. We'd give her a raise too, of course. But someone still needs to do the books and payroll while we are away."

"I can do the accounting. You'll just have to pay for another user for the software, that way I can do it remote if I can't be around. Same goes for payroll."

"Well, that takes care of the store then. What about the house?"

"We'll figure it out, mom. Worst case scenario, I stay here. So, go call Barb and Dick and tell them to get their guest house ready."

****

"Thank you," Mac said as she took the check from Barb. It was the final payment for the work she'd done at the Sandy Shore, she was officially finished there.

"You're more than welcome," Barb said to her. "Thanks to you we're strongly considering leaving the resort open for the winter this year. The numbers you ran and the ideas for specials, fall foliage weekends as an example, piqued my interest and we think we could really keep the place busy. What do you think?"

"Oh, I think you could definitely keep it busy here," Mac said. It was short notice, but the resort had such a great reputation and large enough following that she didn't think the lack of advanced notice mattered. "Just running an ad and emailing all of the past guests would be enough to get the word out, at least in my opinion."

"Great idea! We plan to have Madison manage it, of course."

"She'll do just fine," Mac assured Barb. Mac knew that Mads wanted to run the resort on her own, without her parents breathing down her neck. This would finally be her chance.

"I hope so! We also thought about offering a permanent position to Rylan."

"Permanent?"

"Well, over the winter someone needs to keep the place shoveled and plowed and take care of any repairs that may need to happen. You know how hard it is to find repair men here in the off season. Just the plowing alone could almost be a full-time job, depending on what type of snowfall we get."

"I think it's a great idea. Rylan is a good guy and he's also good at keeping himself busy. Plus, don't forget you've got the nail salon now, so he would need to make sure the walkways are sanded down constantly so no one trips and falls. Overall, I definitely think you need someone paying attention to the outside areas for sure. But hasn't Rylan already taken on another project?" she asked.

"Has he? You know, he did mention to me that he was going to talk to someone down in Wells or York, that big construction company down there. I didn't even think to talk to him about the next steps, now that he's almost done here."

"Well, you might want to talk to him soon," Mac suggested. She couldn't help but think that the apple didn't fall far from the tree, both Mads and her mother seemed to think Rylan was a mind reader and would just stick around Summer Cove forever.

"I'll do it today. Thanks, Mac."

Mac smiled as Barb walked away. She looked at the check, thinking about how she had envisioned taking Rigsy out to a nice fancy dinner when she'd finished her first "real" job. Instead, she'd just get some take out and eat alone while working on the final paperwork for the Van Rohrer's. She paused before leaving the resort, turning around, and walking to Tracy's nail salon.

"Hello?" she asked as she stepped inside.

"Hi!" Tracy said, peeking her head out from behind a large display of nail polish.

"I just happened to be here and wanted to stop by and say hi and see if you had any flyers. I'd be happy to put them up at my parent's store."

"Really? Oh, that'd be great Mac, I really appreciate it," Tracy said, her face lighting up. She walked over to the reception desk and picked up a pile of papers. "Here's some. They also have coupons on them, twenty percent off."

"Great. You'll have no problem getting business at all. Stupid question, though, how do you work on more than one person at a time?"

"Not a stupid question. I have four people that will work for me. Usually they rent a booth, but it's different here. I want to make sure we've got coverage at night."

"Good idea. It looks great, by the way."

"Thanks. Hey, you and Emma and Mads should all come in for mani pedi's some time. My treat."

"Oh, that'd be great," Mac said, taken aback a bit. She wasn't so sure that Mads and Emma would be on board with that, given the history with Tracy. She'd been too busy lately and hadn't even told them yet about their conversation.

"I'd like for things with them to be cool between us. Especially Mads since we're working in the same place. Just an idea."

"I think it's a great idea. I'll talk to them about it and let you know. Thanks!"

She took a left outside of the resort and walked down to the beach, taking off her shoes just to feel the sand between her toes for a few minutes. She needed to get home and work on crunching some numbers but spending a few minutes inhaling the sea air was good for her creativity.

****

"Have you lost your dang mind?"

Mac placed a few chicken wings from the air fryer onto Mads plate before answering. She'd expected both Mads and Emma to balk at the idea of calling a truce with Tracy, and that's exactly what they had done.

"No, I haven't lost my dang mind. Hear me out. It's water under the bridge. Who cares at this point? People deserve second chances, right? I'm not in any way saying that what she did to Emma was okay. But, at the same time, I don't think what Mark did to Emma was okay, and he's back in our friend group and back with Emma."

"Hmm. When you put it that was it's actually a good point, Mac," Mads said. "I guess I have no reason not to be friends with her, or at least cordial. The two of us are going to be working in the same building, after all."

"She's not that bad, either. We had a pretty good talk." Mac left out the part about Tracy's dad, and her being in therapy. That wasn't anyone's business, really, even though Mac did feel that therapy was why Tracy had changed her mind about telling what happened with the guard stand.

"I'm willing to let it go," Emma said as she poured some BBQ sauce on her plate. "Things are going good for me, I don't want to throw bad karma out there. I'm over it."

"Good," Mac said, relieved.

"So, I have some good news. I'm the manager at the store now!" Emma announced.

Mac smiled as she placed some chicken wings on Emma's plate. Emma's smile told her that she was genuinely happy about her parents' decision.

"That's awesome, Em!" Mads said, glancing down at her phone.

"Congrats. It's well deserved, I hope you know that. You're the only person I'd trust to run that place," Mac said.

"Rylan's on his way here," Mads said nervously, standing up and brushing her hair with her hands. "He said he needed to talk to me, unsure about what, but I think I'm going to tell him how I feel."

"Oh jeepers. Here we go," Emma said. "Please, for all of our sakes, tell the kid you like him. Please."

Mac laughed as she nodded her head in agreement.

"You guys need to hide, we need to be alone," Mads said as she ran to the mirror and dabbed on some lip gloss.

"What? No. I'm not hiding in my own apartment," Emma objected.

"Please? Come on, just go in your rooms for a little bit. Please."

"Fine," Emma said, picking her plate up to take with her. "But I'm coming back out here in an hour. You and Rylan can go outside on the deck if you're still talking or whatever it is you need privacy for."

"Tell him," Mac said sternly to Mads as she also left the kitchen and went to her bedroom, just as her phone rang.

"Nice of you to call," Mac said dryly as she flopped down on her bed.

"I knew you'd be mad at me," Rigsy said.

"Well, I haven't heard from you. For all I knew, you were in an accident or something." Mac sat in her bedroom and looked out the window into the cove. She'd bought a new bedroom set with her first check from the Sandy Shore, and the bed had fit perfectly in the bedroom against the back wall. It was high enough that she could sit in bed and still see out the windows into the area below in the cove, and she found herself sitting there and working on her laptop often with the windows open. The sound of the waves along with people milling around helped her focus somehow.

"Mac, you know it's been next to impossible for me to call you. I'd call every day if I could," Rigsy said.

"Okay," she replied curtly.

"Mac, you believe me, right? Please don't be mad at me, I have enough to deal with right now. This place is brutal."

"I have stuff I'm dealing with too, you know," Mac said angrily. "My parents want to go to Florida for the winter, my dad really needs to be in warm weather, and I'd need to stay at their place, and how can I do that and work on growing my business? What if I need to travel? And, business is slow for me, I'm done with the Sandy Shore, and I don't know what's next after I finish the Van Rohrer's. And on top of all of that, I heard that State Troopers don't get to decide where they are stationed the first year of service. When were you going to tell me that?"

"When I got back," Rigsy said, his voice sounding muffled as if he had his hand over the phone. "Mac, I'm really sorry, I have to go. I promise I'll call as soon as I can."

Mac tossed her phone onto her bed in frustration. Her work at Van Rohrer's was almost done and she had nothing else lined up. She'd thought about contacting a few places, making a binder up and showing them what she'd done at her parent's store, the Sandy Shore and Van Rohrer's, but the thought of cold calling people scared her. She didn't want to do it.

As if on cue her phone rang, and she knew by the ring tone that it was Austin. She hesitated, looking at his name on the screen. She had decided to take Mads advice and not talk to him anymore, although she didn't have the guts to tell him that. Instead, she'd just ignored his texts, which was most likely why he was calling her.

The call stopped, and she let out a sigh of relief.

CHAPTER FOURTEEN

Mac brushed the hair off of her face as she stood in the store and looked around.

In a little less than a month she had been able to make noticeable improvements at Van Rohrer's and she was eager for Bob and Mandy to see the store. She and Blaize had asked them not to go there until they'd finished all of the things Mac had been hired to do.

The entire store had been changed around and rebranded. The rear of the store was now for home goods, which were all organized and displayed by category on newly painted black wooden shelves and stands.

The floor had been fixed, the patches had been much lighter than the original floor, so Mac had come up with the idea of laying down grey tile where the replacements needed to be done as well as in other areas, like a random checkboard pattern.

New clothes were starting to arrive and had already been swapped out with the old ones, and the addition of a beauty area held makeup and nail polish, all designer names.

The updated display at the entrance was full of the new items they carried, one of which was Emma's bag, and Mac took a picture to send to Emma.

"Oh, my goodness."

Mac spun around, grinning at the Van Rohrer's.

"What do you think?" she asked.

"This is not what we expected," Mr. Van Rohrer said as he walked around.

"These displays, is everything in them for sale?" Mrs. Van Rohrer asked, sitting down in one of the royal blue velvet armchairs on display.

"Yes. That chair, along with the glass side table, the furry white throw rug, and the faux plant and gold stand can all be bought," Mac said. "By the way, your son designed most of these displays."

"He did?" Mr. Van Rohrer asked, sounding surprised.

"Yes dad, I did," Blaize said as he approached the trio. "I'm not completely useless, you know."

"Oh, stop it you two. This is very impressive, Mac. Oh, wait. Is that Estee Lauder?" Mrs. Van Rohrer asked, walking briskly towards the makeup.

Mac followed Mrs. Van Rohrer over to the newly established makeup section, which had been her favorite to stock.

"Yes. There's Estee, Bobbi Brown, Armani, MAC, just to name a few."

"Oh, good grief, are we making any profit off of this? These prices are more than half off the normal list price."

"Blaize can give you the exact numbers, but off the top of my head I think you're making roughly sixty percent as an average on the makeup," Mac said. "It's a great markup."

Mrs. Van Rohrer raised her eyebrows and nodded her head in approval as she picked up a brow kit from Anastasia Beverly Hills, looking it over before placing it back down and walking towards the front of the store.

"What designer is this?" she asked, picking up the beach bag Emma had made.

"Oh, that's.."

"It's Emma June designs," Blaize said, interrupting Mac. "She's a local designer who makes them by hand."

"Oh, I like this. It's so different. You could use this for so many different things, really. It's roomy but not bulky," Mrs. Van Rohrer held the bag and then placed it on her arm. "It's like a carryall, really. The design I mean. The way it falls. How many of these do we have?"

"Ten," Blaize answered.

"That's all? Why didn't you buy more?"

"Because we don't know if they will sell. If they do, then I will buy more."

"These will sell. In fact, I want this one. I like the color scheme, black with black and white interior and jade green accents. This is really sharp."

Mac watched as Mrs. Van Rohrer walked to the closest mirror and looked at the bag as she held it in various poses.

"It's supposed to be a beach bag, you know," Blaize said to her, laughing.

"Well, it's going to be something different than that for me. I can fit my Yeti tumbler in here, my binder, and other things. It's perfect to use for the office, going back and forth from there to here."

Blaize looked at Mac and rolled his eyes as his mother carried on about the bag.

"I didn't mean to cut you off earlier when she asked who the designer was," Blaize said to Mac as the two watched his mother. "I just didn't want you to mention it was your friend's business. They'd try for a big discount, and your friend is already selling these for less than what she should."

"Thank you," Mac said to him, nodding her head that she understood as his mother approached them.

"Mac, we know it will take months to fully recognize how much revenue your changes have made with the business, but we really like what you've done. The store looks wonderful. Even the outside has changed, it's like a new store. We'd like you to write up another proposal," Mrs. Van Rohrer said to her.

"Another one?" Mac asked.

"Yes. We'd like you to incorporate all of the same changes for all of our stores," Mrs. Van Rohrer said, already placing items from her purse into the bag that she had swiped from the display. "So, we need a proposal to see how much that would be, and the timeline, since it'd be fourteen stores."

"Oh," Mac said, shocked. She found herself getting choked up, she hadn't expected this at all. This was all that she had hoped for, to be given a chance. Fourteen stores! This was huge.

"If you're interested, of course," Blaize said to her, grinning. "You'd have to put up with me."

"I'd love to," Mac said. "There's still a bit of work to be done here, though."

"We know, but what's been done so far is such an improvement, we already agreed that we'd like to do it at every store. How long would it take you to get the proposal to us?" Mr. Van Rohrer asked.

"A few days," Mac said, already running numbers in her head. She could use the same format that she'd used in the first proposal, and plug in the different numbers for each store, but there were unique needs for different regions. "Actually, can we plan on one week? What's popular for a designer in Florida won't necessarily be the same as in New Hampshire, and the different regions have different clothing needs, snow, beach, stuff like that."

"One week is fine, Mac. Thank you," Mrs. Van Rohrer said.

Mac thanked them and said goodbye, leaving the store on cloud nine. As soon as she was in her car she pulled her phone out, eager to text Rigsy. Her smile turned to a frown as she realized that he wouldn't even see it until later that night, or the next day.

She started the car up and drove to the nearest Starbucks, rewarding herself with a victory drink. As she inched forward in the drive-thru her phone dinged, a text from Austin.

Hello? I haven't heard from you

After he had started to flirt with her she'd stopped replying to his texts and answering his calls, but she had a strong urge to tell him about the Van Rohrer's. She knew he'd reply right away if she told him, everyone else was too busy.

They asked me for a proposal to re-brand all of their stores!

She inched her car forward as her phone dinged from an incoming text.

CONGRATULATONS! I knew they would! I'm proud of you! Call me, gorgeous!

She pulled up to the drive-thru window and eagerly took her Frappuccino, a huge smile on her face.

CHAPTER FIFTEEN

"It's going to be a great day, Mac!"

Mac nodded her head at Jim Sousa as she waved
to him. She didn't feel like it was going to be a great
day. It was only seven in the morning, and she was
already in a bad mood, the result of only getting three
hours of sleep. She had already started working on the
new proposals for the Van Rhorer's and it wasn't as cut
and dry as she'd assumed it would be.

Each store had different inventory needs,
different clothing styles, different store layouts.

The big kicker was something that she hadn't even thought of, and it was an issue. She would need to travel extensively to do this job for the Van Rhorer's. And, since there were fourteen stores that needed to be worked on that meant she would be traveling for almost a year. She absolutely wouldn't be able to stay at her parent's house to take care of Muckie and the chickens, and she didn't even know what it meant for her relationship with Rigsy.

"I could kiss you!"

"Huh?" Mac asked Emma, sipping her coffee as Emma stood on the deck, a huge smile on her face. "What'd I do?"

"The bags!"

"Oh, right. Mrs. Van Rohrer loved them. She actually took one from the display to use."

"Mac, they didn't tell you? They want to order two hundred more!"

"Two hundred?" Mac asked, surprised. She knew that they would want to buy more, but thought they wanted to see how well the existing ones sold first and it'd only been a few days that they'd had them.

"Yes! Blaize told me late yesterday, that's why I was out late with Mark. We celebrated. Thank you, this wouldn't have happened without you."

"You're welcome, I'm happy for you. I bet they're sending some down to their stores down south, they have a few near the beaches."

"Maybe, they did order most of them to have a beach accent. I'm just worried about being able to get them all done. I usually make two dozen a week and that's a struggle between my hours at your parent's store and the lack of space here. They don't want them all at once, they want the bulk for December for holiday gifts, but still, it's a lot. How am I ever going to make two hundred?"

Mac didn't say anything, she was worried that the next words to come out of Emma's mouth would be that she might quit working at the store. That would be the cherry on top of the "I have no idea how to help my parents" sundae that Mac was dealing with.

"Anyone want breakfast?" Mads asked as she came outside.

"Let's Door Dash something, my treat," Emma suggested.

"Why are you so happy?" Mads asked.

"I have an order for two hundred of my bags!" Emma said excitedly. "I'm going to order breakfast burritos and iced coffees for us."

"Well, I have some good news, too," Mads said, a huge smile on her face.

"What?" Mac asked.

"My parents want to have the resort stay open for the winter this year. They're going to have me run it alone, and they're hiring Rylan on full time. Which, by the way, is thanks to you Mac."

"I'm so happy that I've helped you guys out," Mac said sarcastically, feeling sorry for herself yet again.

"What's wrong?" Emma asked.

"Yeah, why are you such a crab?" Mads asked, tossing a Cheerio to Sammy, who had landed on the deck and was marching around waiting for his breakfast.

"Gee, I don't know. Could it be because my boyfriend has been away for almost a month now and we have only talked a few times? Or that soon he might be living five hours north of here for a year? Oh wait, maybe it's that my dad's hip is worse than he tells everyone, and he really needs to be in a warm climate, but if I am going to help him make that happen then I can't take the job for the Van Rohrer's."

Emma and Mads stood and stared at Mac as she sat on the deck, leaning back in the chair with her feet up on the deck railing. She didn't look at them, instead she watched as Mike and Mark, Jim Sousa's dogs, bolted towards one of the boats in the cove, practically dragging Jim behind them.

"They asked you to do the rest of their stores? That's awesome!" Mads said.

"Mac, of course you're going to take the gig for the Van Rohrer's. I can cover for your parents at work, no offense to them but I do a lot of it now anyway, they're more involved with talking with the customers. They made me the manager, I totally assumed I'd have more responsibilities," Emma said.

"I know," Mac said sighing heavily. "I'm sorry guys. I didn't mean to sound like such a jerk. It's just that I can't travel, and I'd need to for the Van Rohrer's. I can still do the books for my parents remotely, but someone needs to be at their house, to watch Muckie and get the daily eggs from the chickens. I can't fly to the Van Rohrer's stores if I have to be home every day."

"I'll take Muckie for the winter. He can live at the resort and be the mascot, people will love it. Problem solved," Mads said. "See, wasn't that easy?"

"Thanks, but what about the chickens?" Mac asked. "You know how popular the eggs are at the store."

"I can't do chickens, sorry," Mads joked. "Maybe we can all pitch in somehow, or you can hire someone?"

"I think I have an idea," Emma said slowly.

"What?" Mac asked.

"What if I moved into your parent's house for the winter? I sure could use the extra space for my materials and to make my bags, and I'm sure Mark would have no problem shoveling the driveway and maintaining the place. And we'd take care of the chickens, I can bring the eggs with me to the store every day. Assuming they'd be okay with us staying there, of course."

Mac digested what Emma had just suggested for a few minutes.

"Really?" Mac asked.

"Yes. I really need the extra space to be able to fill the Van Rohrer's order. We have no space here, I've maxed it out. I'm sure you guys are sick of my stuff being all over the place."

"What about when they come back though? You'd have to move back out," Mads asked.

"Mark and I have talked about getting a place together, and this would be perfect as a trial for us. We could just get a place together when your parents come back, or I'd move back in here."

"Are you serious?" Mac asked Emma. "Because this just might work."

"Yes, I'm serious. I need a lot of room to make the bags, and their dining room table would be a huge help, along with all of the living room space. Plus, I could even have Sue from the store help me out, she's been asking for weeks, and I just haven't had the space for her to help out here. I could totally make two hundred bags by the time the Van Rohrer's have asked for them to be done by."

"Well, that sounds like a win-win situation then. Now what about you and Rigsy? The travelling situation for both of you is messed up, how does that get fixed?" Mads asked.

"Sorry, I don't have a solution for that one," Emma said.

Mac sighed. Neither did she.

****

"So, what do you think?" Mac asked her parents as she placed a pile of salad on her dinner plate.

"I knew Emma and Mark were back together. I could tell by the way they looked at each other!" Mac's mother said as she placed a pork chop on Mac's plate.

"Mom, I'm talking about them staying here at the house when you leave for Florida. Emma can also work on her bags here, she'd have Sue from the store help her out. She'd be responsible for the eggs and hens as well."

"I think it's a great idea. We trust Emma, she's got a good head on her shoulders," Mac's father said. "Mark is alright too, I guess."

"Mark is fine," Mac's mom said. "It's a good fix. Emma saved the day, that's for sure."

"Thanks a lot," Mac mumbled. "You know I would stay here if I could. And maybe I can, anyway."

"What's that mean?" her father asked, peeking over the top of the newspaper that he was reading.

"The Van Rohrer's might not want me to do the rest of the stores for all I know. I meet with them tomorrow about it."

"Mackenzie Walsh, stop being so doom and gloom about yourself," Mac's mother said. "Honestly, I don't know what's gotten into you over the last few weeks, but I wish you'd stop."

"Stop what?" Mac asked.

"This is my que to leave," Mac's father said, slowly getting up from his chair in the living room and walking outside with Muckie.

"Mac, you've always been driven. Your father and I have never had to push you, you always pushed yourself. You got yourself into UCLA, for crying out loud! That was all you! And you graduated on time even though you had to drop everything and come back here to help dad and I out when he had his accident. Instead of hanging around here and just babysitting the store look at what you did, you completely changed it. And then, well, I don't know what happened, but your drive kind of…well…stopped."

Mac bit the inside of her cheek as her mother spoke, hating what she'd just heard her say. She hated it because it was true.

"I thought it would be easier, getting customers would be easy," Mac said softly. "I think that's the problem."

"Well, of course you did. Things have been easy for you, for the most part. Sure, you worked hard studying, but you've always been a top student. Even when you don't study you get B's. And you fell into the relationship with Austin almost as soon as you landed in California. So, that was easy. And changing our store? Challenging, but easy, right? You knew the place and the customer base. You know the people."

Mac nodded her head in agreement. They were all valid points.

"I think you got scared," her mother said. "You got scared of having to reach out to people you don't know, to sell yourself. So instead of doing that you just did, well, nothing, unless it fell in your lap. It's also probably why you reached out to Austin. He's familiar, comfortable. You've known Rigsy forever, I know, but this situation with him being away for a month, and starting a career with the State Police is different."

Mac felt ashamed, she'd let herself down and she'd let her parents down.

"Everyone else has their life together, they're growing. Emma wants to manage the store and grow her bag business, and that's happening for her. Mads has always wanted to run the resort alone, and that's happening this winter for her. Rigsy has wanted to be a statie, and that's going to happen. And then there's me, I can't even get my business off the ground unless someone hands me the job."

"That's not true."

"Yes, it is."

"How can you say that when you haven't even tried? How many places have you called?"

Mac shifted in her seat.

"Mac, what I am telling you is you can do it. You will do it. You just have to stop feeling sorry for yourself."

"Thanks mom," Mac said, leaning over to hug her. "I'm going to head home so I can get plenty of sleep. I plan on kicking butt tomorrow with the proposals to the Van Rohrer's!"

CHAPTER SIXTEEN

Mac swore under her breath as she fixed her hair in the Toyota's rearview mirror. She'd decided that if the Van Rohrer's liked her proposal and she got the job the first thing she was doing when she got her first check would be to buy a better vehicle, one that had air conditioning. The humidity had sucked all of the life out of her hair on the drive to the Van Rohrer's, and all that was left now was a mass of frizz.

She pulled her hair as tight as she could into a low bun and got out of the car, carrying one of Emma's bags filled with small binders. For her proposal she had created a binder specifically detailed for each store. It had been a lot of work, but the end result was fantastic.

"Welcome back, Miss Walsh," Jemma said as she greeted Mac at the front door with a warm smile. "They're out back."

"Thanks, Jemma."

Mac made her way through the foyer into the large living room, where there were oversized French doors that led to the back patio. She walked to the area nervously, the sun beating down on her. While it looked professional she wished that she had opted to wear something lighter than her blazer, she was roasting in it.

"Mac! Great to see you. Here, give Bernie your blazer. You must be boiling in it," Mrs. Van Rohrer said.

Mac happily removed the blazer, handing it to Bernie with a smile. "Thank you. I underestimated how strong the sun was today."

"Here, have a seat," Mrs. Van Rohrer said, pointing to the chair next to her, her perfectly manicured nails glistening in the sunlight. They were painted teal green with light gold streaks that sparkled in the sunlight, which would look gaudy on many people but not on her. On her they looked elegant. "Bernie, pour a nice cold glass of lemonade for Mac, would you please."

Mac sat down as Bernie poured her some pink lemonade, nodding her head in thanks to him as she took the glass and sipped on the ice-cold, sweet drink.

"Mac, before we start, we realized that we forgot one thing," Mr. Van Rohrer said to her.

"Oh?"

"References."

"References?" Mac asked. She'd already finished the first store for them, and unless she'd missed something, they were pleased with her work. Why else would they ask her to do the other fourteen stores?

"Yes. Oh, I know we've already had you do one store for us. But the total dollar amount of what we're asking you to do now is quite a lot, at least we assume so based off of the numbers we ran. If we look at what it cost to do one store and estimate each store to cost around the same then it's in the millions. And while that's not your fee, it is what you're recommending. So, we both just want to make sure you can handle such a large and long project," Mrs. Van Rohrer explained.

"The lawyers asked for them," Mr. Van Rohrer added.

"Oh, I see," Mac said. How was she supposed to get referrals when she'd only had one real client, and even then the scope was nothing as big as what she'd be doing for the Van Rohrer's? The self-doubt she'd had crept back into her head, telling her that she'd been right, this was too big of a job for her. The Van Rhorer's weren't sold on her doing it, this proved it.

"I know you did the work on your parent's store, obviously, but what other places have you done? Aside from the Sandy Shore Resort, I mean," Mrs. Van Rohrer asked, picking up a jumbo shrimp from a colorful platter.

"Uh, well, that's it," Mac said, feeling like she wanted to crawl under the table.

"You've only had three customers, and we are one of them?" Mr. Van Rohrer asked, looking over at his wife uneasily.

"Yes. I think we discussed this when we first met though, didn't we?" Mac asked. It wouldn't change anything even if they had, but she was positive that she'd mentioned to them she was just starting out. She hoped they didn't feel like she was trying to trick them, she wasn't at all. Having them ask for references after the fact had blindsided her.

"Oh. Hmm, I don't recall," Mr. Van Rohrer said, briefly scratching his head.

"Hi."

Mac felt a surge of relief as she heard Blaize's voice from behind her. The two had a bumpy start but got along well now, and she hoped that he would put in a good word for her and possibly turn this conversation around. She didn't have any other references, and if that was something the Van Rohrer's needed then this was it, her business was over.

As she turned to say hello to Blaize her jaw dropped.

"Tracy?"

"Hi Mac! Good to see you."

"You two know each other?" Mrs. Van Rohrer asked, surprised.

"I told you that mother. She introduced Tracy and I, remember?" Blaize said, sighing.

"Oh, that's right, you did tell me that."

"Mac, when do you start on the next store? Which one will it be, anyway?" Blaize asked her, swiping a grape from the fruit platter.

"Oh, well, I suggested in my proposal that the New Hampshire location be next, and I work my way down south, but there's a slight issue," Mac said.

"What issue?"

"Your mother and I need some references, that's all," Mr. Van Rohrer said, waving his hand to shoo a bug away.

"References? She already did the store for you, shouldn't you have asked about references before she did it? What's the point now?" Blaize asked.

"Well, Blaize, the point is that Josh brought up the fact that with a job as big as this, which is basically re-branding all of our stores, we should have references for Mac," Mr. Van Rohrer explained.

"Josh, of course," Blaize rolled his eyes. "Dad, Josh is a legal guy. He's always asking for things like this just so you cover your butt, you know that."

"Well, that's because it's his job, Blaize. We need to protect ourselves," Mrs. Van Rohrer said, holding her glass up for a refill.

"Mac did a great job at the Sandy Shore," Tracy said, stepping closer to the table. "I wouldn't have my salon if it weren't for her."

"Is that so?" Mrs. Van Rohrer asked, eying Tracy.

"It sure is," Tracy confirmed, smiling at Mac.

Mac watched as Mrs. Van Rohrer looked at her own nails and realized that Tracy had most likely done Mrs. Van Rohrer's nails at the salon. She'd had flyers made up all over town and run an ad in the coastal paper, everyone knew about the new nail salon that was inside of the resort.

"Well, I wasn't aware that the nail salon had been something you'd come up with for the Sandy Shore," she said, still looking at her nails. "It's going to be a gold mine."

"Yes, especially since it will be open year-round now," Mac said. "I met with the owners a few days ago with suggestions on fall foliage specials they can run on the rooms and other ideas for the off season."

"She knows what she's doing, see?" Blaize said to his parents, winking at Mac.

"Oh my, the Sandy Shore is staying open this winter? That's wonderful. We should connect and have a coupon for the rooms, so they can do some shopping while they're here. You know, people love to shop off season. Well, knowing this, I don't think we need referrals then, do we Bob? Like Blaize said, she's already done one store for us, and we are happy with the results so far. And her work at the Sandy Shore is excellent, I saw it when I was there getting my nails done," Mrs. Van Rohrer said.

"Mandy, you and Josh are the ones who started up about references to begin with," Bob said, rolling his eyes at her. "You agreed with Josh."

Mac shifted in her seat uneasily, feeling as if everyone was unaware that she was still sitting there. She was starting to sweat, and no amount of pink lemonade was going to stop her because it was more from nerves than anything.

"Mom, it's a hundred degrees out here, give Mac a break, would ya?" Blaize asked.

"Mac, I'm sorry. We just got a bit nervous, Josh can be really pushy at times and overly cautious. If we really had a concern we should have asked before you started on the first store, like Blaize said. I'm sorry. Are those binders for us?"

"Yes, each store has a proposal in a different binder," Mac said, feeling relieved. She'd dodged a huge bullet.

She handed a binder to the Van Rohrer's as Blaize and Tracy said goodbye, and started on her sales pitch, thankful that the crisis had been averted. Making amends with Tracy had definitely worked in her favor.

****

"You're getting spoiled," Mac said as she placed the bowl of Cheerios down on the deck for Sammy. The seagull cocked his head sideways and looked at her before hopping down on the deck to eat.

She'd gotten home from the Van Rohrer's hours earlier and was waiting to hear if they wanted to move ahead with her proposal or not. In the interim, as a precaution, she was applying for an increase on her credit card, as she'd realized that flights and hotel costs while working at the different stores would add up and she would need more than the five-thousand-dollar limit that she currently had.

She looked up as she heard a car horn blaring and watched as Mads drove through slowly through the cove, the crowds of people moving out of her way. Mac looked at her watch. It was three and Mads usually worked at the resorts front desk until seven or eight at night on Friday's because it was the busiest day of the week at the resort. Hearing the car door slam she winced and walked into the living room, mentally preparing herself for whatever drama was about to happen.

The door flung open and Mads stormed in, tossing her keys on the kitchen counter before opening the refrigerator and pulling out a Truly, opening up the alcoholic beverage and drinking down half of it in one gulp.

"Uh, bad day?" Mac asked cautiously.

"Rylan's leaving," Mads said as she walked out to the deck.

Mac hesitated, unsure if she should follow her friend outside or not. Mads was obviously upset, maybe she just wanted to sit outside and be alone.

"He leaves next week!" Mads yelled from the deck, a cue to Mac that she wanted to talk.

Mac grabbed herself a Truly from the refrigerator and stepped outside, sitting down next to Mads.

"What happened? Last I knew you were supposed to tell him how you felt the other day when he came over, and your mom was offering him a permanent job at the resort."

"She did. He already accepted the one down in York," Mads said, finishing her Truly and then reaching out for the one Mac had.

"Oh. I'm sorry, Mads. I had kinda assumed that he would stay after you talked to him. Maybe the job in Wells is better for him long term? It's not that far away from Summer Cove, you two could still have a relationship, right? Is that the plan?"

"I didn't tell him," Mads said, taking a sip of Mac's Truly.

"You didn't tell him what, exactly?"

"I told him that he should stay but didn't exactly say that it was because I had feelings for him. I just said that we would have fun."

"Hold on a minute. When he came over here the other day what did he want?" Mac asked.

"Uh, he wanted to tell me that he had an awesome summer with me and hoped that we'd continue it."

"And you said what to him?"

"I told you, I said we'd have fun if he stayed," Mads said, tossing a dirty look at Sammy, who was stomping around on the deck.

"Mads, I'm not even in the relationship and I am confused so I can imagine how Rylan feels. You're still giving him friend vibes. If he likes you more than as a friend, and thinks you don't feel the same way, why would he want to stay here? It would be torture working with the person you're in love with every day when they don't feel the same way. I thought you were going to tell him how you felt, we've had this conversation way too many times."

"I'm scared to," Mads said softly. "I'm not like you and Emma."

"What's that mean?" Mac asked. "What are we like?"

"I've never told a guy that I love them before. You and Emma have been in serious relationships, I haven't. Ever. Everyone our age has been in love before except for me. I'm a loser."

Mac couldn't believe what she was hearing. Mads was a popular person in Summer Cove, all the guys liked her, and they always had since the two were kids. She was the spunky one out of the Summer Cove girls, the dare devil. Nothing ever seemed to bother her, she always had a smile on her face and didn't put up with anyone's crap. She was strong, and to hear her say she was a loser was something Mac had never once thought about her in a million years.

"Knock it off, Mads. You are not a loser! You haven't ever been in a serious relationship by choice, your choice. And now you're so afraid of rejection that you won't even tell Rylan the truth about how you feel, even though it's so obvious to all of us that he likes you. Please tell him."

"What if he doesn't, though?"

"Doesn't what? Feel the same way? Well, then it is what it is, but at least you won't sit around all day wondering what if. If you don't tell him you will never know. Sometimes you just have to push yourself outside of your comfort zone, put yourself out there."

"Rip it off like a band aid, I guess," Mads said as she stood up. "Thanks."

"Go tell him. Like, now," Mac said, laughing. "Because I will kill you if we have to have this same convo again."

"I will. I promise. How'd the meeting go, did you get the big job?"

"I'm still waiting to hear, but I think it went well. I've been pacing around all day, I'm going to eat dinner at my parents just to get my mind off of it."

"Gotchya. Hey, when's Rigsy back, isn't it soon?"

"He was supposed to call and tell me, I thought it was the end of this week, but I haven't heard from him as usual," Mac shrugged. She'd lost track of the days over the past week and wasn't sure when Rigsy was coming back, and she wasn't going to stress over it. She had enough other things to stress over.

CHAPTER SEVENTEEN

Mac squinted her eyes as she pulled into her parent's driveway. There was a black car parked in it that she wasn't familiar with, and she groaned as she looked down at her outfit. She'd thrown on ripped jean shorts and a T-shirt, expecting to have a casual dinner with just her parents, not anyone else.

She turned the corner to the back of the house and gasped.

"Hi."

She screeched and ran over to Rigsy, hugging him as he picked her up and spun her around. She had no idea that he'd be there, or that he was even coming home.

"I wanted to surprise you," he said to her.

"Well, you did! When did you get back?" she asked, hugging him again.

"Only an hour ago. I called your parents early this morning so I could surprise you. Plus, I really wanted some of your moms home made cookies, I've had nothing but vending machine food for dessert all month."

Mac's mom smiled as she pointed to dozens of chocolate chip cookies, layer bars and lemon bars that she'd baked.

"Well, it looks like my mom made enough for you for a month," Mac joked. "Thanks mom."

"We've got burgers and hot dogs, and a nice thick ribeye for Rigsy," Mac's father said, pointing to the steak. "The best for the best!"

Mac groaned as Rigsy laughed. Her parents were so proud of Rigsy. She loved that they were so supportive of him.

"Mac, can you go get the mustard and ketchup?" her mom asked as she fussed over the food that her dad was taking off of the grill. "Rigsy, what do you want on your steak?"

"I'll have some of this," Rigsy said, picking up the BBQ sauce on the picnic table and shaking the bottle, unaware that the cover wasn't on it tightly. The cover flew off, and BBQ sauce spilled all over his chest and arms.

"Oh no," Mac's mom said. "I'll go get paper towels!"

"No, it's fine. I'll take care of it, Mrs. Walsh. Mac let's go grab some stuff," Rigsy said to Mac, nodding his head towards the house. She followed him inside where he immediately pulled her towards him, kissing her.

"I missed you," she said, the butterflies in her stomach still fluttering from the kiss.

"I missed you too. I'm gonna go clean up, I'll be right back. Uh, you might want to wipe your shirt off."

Mac giggled as she looked down and saw BBQ sauce on her shirt. She dabbed at it with paper towels as she opened the refrigerator and pulled out the ketchup and mustard.

"What's this?"

Looking up over the refrigerator door she saw Rigsy standing in the living room, holding something up.

It was the envelope with the letter that Austin had sent her. She'd left it on her nightstand weeks ago when she had read it.

"Oh, uh, it's nothing," she answered, trying to act casual despite her heart beating so loud that she was sure Rigsy could hear it. She wanted to run.

"If it was nothing then you wouldn't have bothered to save it."

"I meant to throw it away, that's why it's all wrinkled up. It's not a big deal, really."

"It kind of is a big deal. I didn't think you still talked to him."

"I don't. He mailed the letter here to my parent's house because I'd blocked him on everything."

"He must have had something really important to tell you, sending you a letter," Rigsy said.

Mac didn't answer him. She didn't want to tell him what the letter said, and definitely didn't want him to read it. She wanted to kick herself for not throwing it away. Why had she saved it?

"Have you talked to him?" Rigsy asked.

Mac's heart sunk. She didn't want to answer that question because it was open ended.

"Mac? Have you?"

"Yes," she answered, sighing. "But please hear me out. I was having a difficult day, and I couldn't talk to you, and I was upset. And we haven't talked about anything inappropriate at all, we are just friends."

The hurt look on Rigsy's face told her all that she needed to know, and her shoulders sank. She felt like a real jerk. Without saying anything Rigsy dropped the envelope on the kitchen table and walked out the door.

"Did Rigsy just leave?" her mom asked, a confused look on her face as she came inside.

Mac burst into tears as she sat down at the table, the envelope lying in front of her like a bad omen.

"Oh Mac, did he see this?" her mother asked, holding up the letter.

"Yes. He saw it and he knows I have been talking to Austin." Tears rolled down Mac's face as Muckie came clamoring through his doggie door and ran over to her, putting his head on her lap.

"Are you back together with Austin?" her mother asked, handing her a tissue.

"What? No! Mom, jeez. I love Rigsy. I was just feeling sorry for myself I guess, Rigsy was gone and Emma and Mads are always with their boyfriends and mine was gone. And I have thought a few times about how I left things with Austin, just walking out. Even though it ended bad for the most part the four years we were together were good, he isn't a bad guy or anything. And, I guess what you said before, about him being comfortable to me, played a role, too."

"I see," her mother said. "So, you have no interest in Austin at all? You just wanted to get a bit of closure, along with some attention perhaps?"

"That sounds horrible," Mac groaned. "I don't want to be with Austin, mom. If I did I would be. Yes, I needed some attention, I guess. I just had so much going on with the Van Rohrer's, and you and dad, and everything else, I needed someone to talk to."

"You shouldn't be telling me this, you should be telling Rigsy," her mother said. "Mac, I know the past few weeks have been difficult for you. But you're not a little kid anymore. This is the real world, adulthood. You have to learn to roll with the punches, in this case learn to cope or pick better in terms of who's shoulder you want to cry on when your boyfriend is away."

Mac sunk down in her chair, tears falling down her cheeks again. Her mother was right. Talking to Austin was attention seeking and she shouldn't have done it. She needed to apologize to Rigsy and hope that he forgave her.

***

"So, we can't be friends anymore? This is kind of childish."

Mac paced around her bedroom as she talked to Austin, pausing to look out her window every few minutes. She hadn't heard from Rigsy since he had left her parents house hours earlier, he hadn't answered his phone or replied to her texts. In the interim she'd called Austin to tell him that she wouldn't be able to talk to him every day like they had been, and he wasn't handling it well.

"Yes, we can still be friends. You know why we can't talk every day, Austin."

"Actually, I don't. It isn't like our conversations are inappropriate, right?"

Mac paused before answering. If she was going to be honest yes, some of them had been inappropriate. Maybe it was on the very edge, but still. More than once recently, Austin had brought up things they had done in the past, a date they'd had that wound up with them skinny dipping, the Ferris wheel getting stuck while they were on it and fireworks going off while they were stuck at the top, things that she wouldn't want Rigsy reliving with any of his exes. Then there were his recent texts, where he would always add "gorgeous" or "beautiful" when texting her. She knew if she mentioned any of this to Austin he would laugh it off and tell her that she was being dramatic.

"Right. It's just that we've been talking and texting every day, and I need to focus on work. Plus, my boyfriend Rigsy is back now, and I don't think he'd be thrilled if he and I are together, and my ex is texting me memes that are inside jokes or calling me at midnight. You wouldn't like that, right? If the situation were reversed?"

"I wouldn't be controlling."

Mac laughed. To think that Rigsy was controlling was a stretch, a big one. He would never tell her that she couldn't talk to Austin, he was upset because she did it behind his back. And the truth was that she had been spending too much time goofing off talking to Austin when she should have been focusing on finding new clients.

"I don't know why you'd say anything about controlling, and if you're suggesting that Rigsy asked me not to talk to you you're wrong. Like I said, I need to focus more on work and my relationship, and less on chatting with my ex. Don't make me out to be a bad guy in this, please."

"Whatever you say, Mackenzie. I'll wait to hear from you."

She looked at her phone screen to confirm that he'd ended the call so abruptly. He had. She wasn't sure if she should be relieved that she'd told him or angry that he had reacted the way that he had. Either way, she was positive that she'd learned a lesson, trying to be just friends with your ex wasn't a good idea.

CHAPTER EIGHTEEN

"Those heaters are awfully big."

Mac ignored Verna Nixon as she stood next to Emma, watching the delivery of the outdoor patio heaters. There were six of them, each of them eight feet tall. They'd throw off enough heat to allow for outdoor seating well into November, possibly even later.

"They look good, don't you think?" Emma asked Mac. "I think we should add some decorations around the base, you know, pumpkins and mums or something."

"Sure," Mac replied unenthusiastically, turning to enter the store. She needed more caffeine, despite already having three large tumblers of coffee that morning. She stepped behind the counter and started to pour herself more cold brew, yawning.

"I'll take an extra-large."

Mac spun around, knocking her tumbler over in the process and spilling her iced coffee all over the floor.

"Hi," she mumbled to Rigsy. "Give me a minute."

She threw a bunch of paper towels down on the floor to cover the mess and reached into the cooler to grab the container of cold brew. She filled a cup with ice and then poured the cold brew in.

"Three sugars," Rigsy said as she placed the cover on.

"Since when do you take sugar in your coffee?" Mac asked him, taking the cover off and pouring sugars in before mixing it up.

"I guess a few things changed while I was away," Rigsy said to her, taking the cup. "Thank you."

She watched as he threw a five-dollar bill down on the counter and walked away.

"Well, that wasn't awkward or anything," Emma said as she stepped behind the counter. "Any idea when you two will be making up? Because this is getting super weird to be around."

Mac agreed, it was super weird. She and Rigsy hadn't talked much at all since he had found the letter a few days ago. Mac had tried to explain to him that she was sorry, but he hadn't wanted to listen. She felt horrible but was also starting to get angry over the situation. Did Rigsy want to break up over this? Were they already broken up? What was going on with the State Police, where was he going to be stationed? How would she know any of this if the only time he spoke to her was to get his coffee?

"Look at this! We have a celebrity here!"

Mac looked up as Nixon Woods, a local who's head was always buried in the newspaper, waved the mornings paper around.

"Who?" Emma asked.

"Who? Our very own Mac!"

"Huh?" Mac asked, taking the paper out of Nixon's hands.

On the front page was an article about Van Rohrer's being reborn, along with a photo of Mac, Blaize and Mr. and Mrs. Van Rhorer standing in front of the store. One of the employees had taken the picture, she'd asked them to and had printed it up and framed it for the Van Rohrer's.

"Oh wow, I didn't know anything about this article," Mac said, grinning as she started to read it. The Van Rohrer's had mentioned meeting with a reporter, but Mac knew that was common and hadn't thought her name would even be mentioned in their discussion. She was thrilled to be included in it.

"It says you're going to be remodeling all of their stores because you did such a good job with the one here. I was just there last night, I had my niece with me, and she must have bought the entire makeup department! Congratulations Mac!"

"Thanks," Mac said, her face turning red from embarrassment. Her mood lifted a bit, raised by the cheers and accolades coming from the customers.

She just wished that Rigsy had been there to see it.

****

"Who would ever think this would be happening?" Emma asked as she held her hand out in front of her, wiggling her fingers.

"Not me!" Mads joked.

"Thanks again, Tracy. I think it's cool we are doing this," Mac said as she took a sip of her champagne while waiting for her nails to dry. Tracy had shut the salon down so that it was just them, aside from her staff. It was a nice, relaxing time and they'd had some great laughs.

"So, Mac, any idea where Rigsy will be stationed yet?" Tracy asked.

"I don't think so," Mac said, wiggling her freshly painted toes.

"Jeez, you'd think they would tell him by now. He starts soon, right? I think he told me two weeks?"

"He told you? When?" Mac asked.

"Last week when he texted me about the handicapped space for my grandmother. I forgot he was away when I asked, otherwise I wouldn't have bothered him."

"You and Rigsy text each other?" Mads asked, looking at Mac and raising her eyebrows.

"Well, kind of. We've always stayed in touch, I mean we grew up together, remember? Every now and then when something comes up we'll shoot each other a text, sure. Oh Mac, you aren't mad, are you?" Tracy asked, a worried look on her face.

Mac wasn't sure if she was mad or not. Rigsy had certainly never told her that he and Tracy texted each other.

"Here, look at my phone," Tracy said, handing her phone over to Mac. "I don't want you thinking we're being sketchy. See, the last text was him asking about the properties up north that my stepfather owns. One of his new friends from the academy needed a place to rent."

Mac took the phone and scanned through the texts. They were infrequent, only a few for the entire year, and completely mundane. Just as Tracy had said. She handed the phone back to Tracy.

"It's fine. I don't care if you guys talk, really. We had an argument a few days ago over me talking to my ex, so I guess I'm just surprised that he would get so mad at me when he's basically doing the same thing."

"Well, hold on. There's a big difference between you talking to Austin and Rigsy talking to Tracy," Emma said.

"How?" Mac asked.

"For starters, you and Austin had a relationship for four years. You lived together. Tracy and Rigsy lasted all of four minutes, it wasn't serious," Emma said. "No offense, Tracy."

"None taken," Tracy replied.

"Well, yes, but so what? Why is it okay for Rigsy to text an ex, and not for Mac to? That's kind of hypocritical, isn't it?" Mads questioned.

"Exactly!" Mac said in agreement. "He's giving me the cold shoulder when he's done the same exact thing."

"I feel terrible," Tracy said, slugging back her champagne.

"Don't, this isn't your fault," Mac said. She drank her champagne and thought of how she'd approach Rigsy about this and what his reaction would be. Hopefully, he'd agree that he had overreacted and that would be that, things would go back to normal. The key word was hopefully.

CHAPTER NINETEEN

"Hiya, Mac!"

Mac nodded her head to Celeste and made her way through the crowd to the bar at Russo's, sitting at the very end and ordering a vodka tonic.

"Meeting anyone?" Bryan asked as he slid her glass over to her.

"Yeah, me. I'll take a beer. Thanks, Bryan," Rigsy said as he sat down next to Mac.

"Thanks for coming," Mac said, swiveling in her bar stool to face him. He had just gotten off shift and was still in uniform, which was rare. He almost always changed before going out, but she'd also emphasized that she wanted to talk to him as soon as possible.

"We do need to talk, I agree," he said. "I just needed some space."

"Well, it's been almost a week," Mac said. "And to be honest, now I'm the one who's upset."

"Why?" Rigsy asked her.

"You're a hypocrite."

"Huh?"

"You were mad at me for talking to Austin, but you talk to Tracy."

"It's not remotely the same, Mac."

"Really, how?"

"Well, for starters, I didn't have a serious relationship with Tracy. And, you know we text. All of us from school do, just because you stopped doesn't mean everyone else had to. Yesterday Christine Ryder texted me because she got a ticket."

Christine was a girl they'd gone to school with, someone Mac saw around town every now and then. Along with a lot of the other kids they had grown up with.

"Rigsy, you know what I mean about being a hypocrite. I didn't know you talked to Tracy. And you didn't even let me explain about Austin."

"Well, I know that I'm not in love with Tracy," Rigsy said, taking a sip from his beer.

"So, you did read the letter, didn't you?" Mac asked. He had said he didn't, but she knew he must have. Otherwise, why would he say that, about not being in love?

"Yes, I did. Do you understand why I am so upset, why I needed space? It's kind of a kick in the pants, to be away and find out that your girlfriend has been talking to her ex the whole time, the ex who wants her back."

Mac turned her stool so that she faced forward and sat in silence. She was upset that he'd lied about reading the letter, upset that he read it in the first place. It was an invasion of her privacy. At the same time, would she do the same if the situation were reversed? She hated to admit it, but she probably would. And she'd be just as crushed as Rigsy was.

"I guess maybe we both need space," Rigsy said as he stood up. He placed enough money on the bar for both of their drinks and a generous tip and left, leaving Mac even more confused and upset than she'd been when she got there.

****

Mac eagerly opened the envelope that the Fed Ex guy had dropped off to her at the apartment. She'd received a call from Mrs. Van Rohrer that they wanted to go ahead with her proposal, and that she'd sent along paperwork for her to get the ball rolling.

She pulled out the contract that the Van Rohrer's had drawn up with their lawyer and scanned it over. Mads had given her the name of a lawyer that she could send the contract to, just to ensure there wasn't anything in it that she should change. On the surface it looked fine to her.

There was a company credit card inside with her name on it, which she found odd as they hadn't discussed that when they had spoken.

She called Mrs. Van Rohrer while holding the card, flipping it over between her fingers.

"Hi Mrs. Van Rohrer, it's Mac. Yes, I did get the envelope, thank you. I have one question though. There's a company credit card inside of it?"

"Oh, yes Mac. That's for all of your incidentals, it's easier for both of us. This way all of your travel charges can be put on the company card, and we can pay it directly for you."

"Oh, that's perfect! Thanks so much," Mac said, a huge wave of relief washing over her. She'd been worried about how she could juggle the cost of travel since her credit card company hadn't given her the increase on her line that she'd requested.

"Is everything still on schedule for you to start on October first?"

"Yes. I look forward to it," Mac said enthusiastically.

"Great! We'll be in touch."

Mac looked at the card as she ended the call, placing it down when she heard Sammy screeching out on the deck. She grabbed the box of Cheerios that they kept on the counter and walked out onto the deck.

"You know, I'm not going to be here much starting next month. Who's going to feed you when I'm gone?" she tossed some Cheerios towards the seagull, and Sammy eagerly ate them up.

She threw some more down and leaned up against the deck railing, looking out at the cove. It was the first week of September, although weather wise nothing had changed. The days had still been hot, and the nights were getting cooler. Labor Day weekend was approaching, signaling the end of summer, although the crowds had already decreased significantly because some schools had already started for the year.

She heard someone calling her name and looked down. Mads was walking towards the cove with Rylan. She waved, then let out a loud "WOOT WOOT!" as she saw the two of them were holding hands. Mads must have finally told Rylan how she felt, all summer long the only time she had allowed PDA was at last call. She grinned, happy for Mads. Things had fallen into place for both Emma and Mads that summer, that was for sure.

She sighed as she thought about herself. Her business had finally taken off as far as she was concerned. But her love life was up in the air, and that wasn't something she had thought would have happened. She had no idea if Rigsy would forgive her. She had no idea where he was going to be stationed, or when he would even start with the State Police.

She walked back into the apartment, not allowing herself to dwell on the things that she couldn't control. She needed to get the contract looked at by her attorney so she could sign it, and then start to plan her trips to the Van Rhorer's stores. If Rigsy wanted to talk, he knew where to find her. Until he did she'd move ahead with her life. What else could she do?

CHAPTER TWENTY

The flames from the bon fire danced twenty feet in the air as crowds of people milled around on the beach, drinking the Sandy Shore resorts famous "Bon Fire Booze", a special mix of rum, pineapple juice and Sprite with a dash of Fireball.

"Are the flames supposed to be that high?" Mark asked Rylan nervously.

"No, they should be higher," Rylan joked, laughing. "Don't worry, it's surrounded by sand, I won't burn the town down."

Mac held onto her red plastic Solo cup as she walked towards the resort. It was the perfect evening for the annual town bonfire, a crisp clear night. Food trucks had set up in the parking lot and there were activities all down the beach sponsored by the resort as well as local businesses.

"I'm sorry Rigsy isn't here, I know you must be upset," Mac's mom said to her as she fussed with the desserts on the table. "Here, have a brownie."

"I'm not hungry, thanks," Mac said, stepping aside so a group of people could take some of the desserts on the table.

"Hi Mac!"

Mac turned to face Tracy, grinning as she saw Blaize next to her.

"Hi guys. Good to see you," Mac said. "Mom, this is Blaize Van Rohrer, the General Manager I worked with."

"Oh, Blaize! Yes, I heard a lot about you. Here, have a seven-layer bar. Tracy, you take one too. You're so thin, you should take a brownie, too."

"Your daughter did a great job at the store, we're all excited for her to do it with all of the others," Blaize said to Mac's mom.

"We are very proud of her!" Mac's mom said.

"Thanks," Mac said, trying to sound grateful and not morose, which was how she felt. This wasn't how she had pictured her summer ending.

She walked towards the far end of the beach, wanting to sit alone for a bit. Everyone was in a great mood except for her. She hadn't heard from Rigsy, nor had she reached out to him. She guessed that it was over for them, which wasn't what she wanted but she'd accepted it. Soon she would be traveling anyway, she wouldn't have time for a relationship.

"Mind if I join you?"

She looked up at Rigsy and shrugged, trying not to let him see that she was surprised that he was there. Her heart started to beat faster, and the butterflies kicked up in her stomach.

"It's a perfect night for the bonfire," he said, looking up at the sky that was littered with stars.

"Yeah, it is," Mac replied.

"I found out where I'll be stationed," Rigsy said. "I'll be in Lincoln."

"Oh, cool," Mac replied. She didn't know what to say to him. Lincoln was four hours away from Summer Cove.

"Mac, is this really what you want? Because it isn't what I want. I leave in two days, and I think we should talk about us."

"Is there an us?"

"Well, I'd like to think that there is. I've been mad, maybe I overreacted but that doesn't mean what you did was okay," Rigsy said.

"You're a hypocrite. You blew up on me because I was talking to Austin and the whole time you were doing the same thing with Tracy."

"There's a difference, Mac."

"No, there isn't."

"Austin still loves you. Tracy and I were never even in love. We really are just friends. Can you say the same about you and Austin?"

Mac didn't answer Rigsy. He had made a valid point.

"The letter he sent you, he wanted you back, right? I didn't read it all the way through. I didn't have to. So, that's why I reacted how I did, Mac. You knew he wanted you back and you still talked to him. How was I supposed to feel?"

"You didn't even let me explain myself, you just automatically assumed. Why didn't you give me a chance to talk to you about it? What did I ever do that led you to not trust me?"

"Mac, you left Summer Cove and never looked back. You met Austin and had a whole new life out in California. He's rich and well educated, I can't compete with that. And when you came back you said you wanted nothing to do with him ever again, but here you are. Talking to him. Maybe that is the life you want, back with him. That's how I felt."

"That's ridiculous, Rigsy. I stayed here because this is where I want to be, in Summer Cove. I talked to him because I felt alone, I guess. You were gone, and Mads and Emma had Rylan and Mark, and I made a bad decision."

They sat in silence for what seemed like hours, the sound of the waves crashing and the crowds at the bonfire in the distance. A cold breeze blew in, and Mac shivered. She'd only worn a thin short sleeve T-shirt and had left her sweater in the car.

"Here," Rigsy said, taking his sweater off and giving it to her.

She put his sweater on, immediately feeling warm. The arm length was longer than her arms were and if she stood up she knew the sweater would fall a bit above her knees. She loved wearing his clothes, they made her feel safe, they made her feel content. Without even thinking she put her head on his shoulder as they continued to look out at the ocean.

"Lincoln is only an hour away from Bangor, you know. You said you would be flying every week."

"I will be. Well, after I finish the New Hampshire store," Mac said.

"Bangor is an international airport, it isn't a small local one like we have here. There are daily flights from every major airport. You could fly there when I have my two days a week off and we could stay at a hotel or something. Or I could fly to you sometimes. I looked up the Van Rohrer store locations and they're all in major cities, major airports. It isn't like I am afraid to leave the state of Maine, you know. We could make it work if you wanted to."

"You looked up all the store locations?" Mac asked, her heart melting.

"Yeah. I mapped it all out the other day," Rigsy replied sheepishly.

"You get two days a week off? I figured you'd have to work crazy shifts like you do here," Mac said, reaching for his hand.

"It's different with the state, at least that's what all the guys have told me. Overtime isn't mandatory. I get two days a week off, but it could be midweek one week and then a weekend the next."

"And you would be willing to fly to where I am?" Mac asked, giggling. Rigsy was afraid to fly.

"Yes," he said, laughing. "As long as you can get me some anxiety pills. But I won't have most weekends off, being the new guy. And I wouldn't want to interrupt your schedule, flying in midweek."

"I choose when I want to work, so I have a lot of flexibility," Mac said, her mind spinning.

A loud boom interrupted them, the annual fireworks had started. They watched the display, the sky lighting up over the water with reds, greens, and blues.

"You leave in two days, is that what you said?" Mac asked.

"Yes."

She leaned over and kissed him, just as the finale for the fireworks blasted overhead.

"Well, then I guess we should head back to my place so we can be alone for the next two days. Oh, and so we can sign you up for a frequent flyer card, you're going to be doing a lot of traveling soon!"

THE END

If you enjoyed this series you'll love my others!

The Cottage on Grasshopper Lane

Available in paperback and eBook

Amazon, Barnes & Noble

Crosby's Cove

Available in paperback and eBook

Amazon, Barnes & Noble

Thank you for purchasing this book and supporting an independent author!

Author Catherine Jones 2022 ©